DISNEY PRESENTS A PIXAR FILM

THE INCREDIBLES

The Junior Novelization

 Published in the United States by Random House Children's Books, a division of Random House, Inc., New York, and simultaneously in Canada by Random House of Canada Limited, Toronto, in conjunction with Disney Enterprises, Inc. RANDOM HOUSE and colophon are registered trademarks of Random House, Inc.

Library of Congress Control Number: 2004103549

ISBN: 0-7364-2215-3

The term OMNIDROID used by permission of Lucasfilm Ltd.

The text of this book is set in 13-point Times Ten.

www.randomhouse.com/kids/disney

Printed in the United States of America
10 9 8 7 6 5 4 3

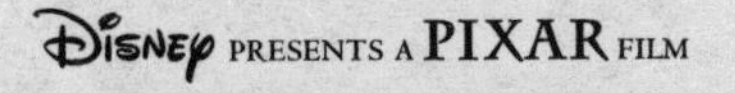

THE INCREDIBLES

The Junior Novelization

Adapted by Irene Trimble

Chapter 1

The sun was just beginning to set over the city of Municiburg. A powerfully built, handsome blond bachelor wearing a tuxedo maneuvered his sporty little car through the streets of the city, listening to the radio. He was on his way to a very important appointment, when suddenly—

"We interrupt for an important bulletin!" The man listened for details. A high-speed car chase between police and gunmen was in progress on San Pablo Boulevard.

Without hesitation, the man punched a button on the dash. The radio immediately converted into an electronic aerial map. The map's sophisticated radar system locked on two red dots speeding through the city. "Yeah, I've got time," the man decided, giving his watch a glance. He could still make his appointment.

He hit another button, marked AUTODRIVE, and the car began to drive itself. Then he typed MERGE PURSUIT into the controls. The autodrive immediately began to plot a course to intercept the trouble.

Next, the seat backs of the car snapped down flat. Two steel bands suddenly wrapped around the man's waist and slid over his body in opposing directions, removing his clothes to reveal a slick Super suit underneath. He wore a dark mask over his eyes.

The seat backs returned to an upright position. The man in the driver's seat was none other than Mr. Incredible. And he was ready for action!

Mr. Incredible smiled as his vehicle converted into the sleek futuristic Incredibile. As he hit the turbo button, afterburners flamed and the car rocketed down the street.

Then something caught his eye.

A sweet gray-haired woman was frantically waving at him and pointing at a tree. Mr. Incredible hit the brakes, reverse retro-thrusters fired, and the Incredibile stopped on a dime. A darkly tinted window slid down. "What is it, ma'am?"

"My cat, Squeaker, won't come down," she cried.

Mr. Incredible glanced up at the wild-eyed Squeaker, who was stubbornly gripping the tree, then at the screen on the dash of the Incredibile. Red dots from the car chase were now headed their way. A blazing car-to-car gun battle would rip down this street within moments.

"I suggest you stand clear," he said to the cat's owner. "There could be trouble."

Suddenly, the squeal of screeching tires could be heard. The headlights of the cars were moving toward them fast. In one sweeping motion, Mr. Incredible tore the enormous tree out of the ground and gently shook Squeaker into his owner's outstretched arms. Then he slammed the tree onto the hood of the oncoming car, stopping the criminals in their tracks.

As he carefully replanted the tree, Mr. Incredible accepted the usual thanks from the police. "Just here to help," he said, giving each of them a nod. "Officers, ma'am . . . Squeaker." He was about to leave the scene when the radio began to blare, "Tour bus robbery in the vicinity of Howard and Chase streets."

Mr. Incredible looked at his watch again. *I've still got time,* he thought, deciding to take the call. He jumped into the Incredibile, but just before he pulled out, someone *in* the car said, "Cool! Ready for takeoff!"

Mr. Incredible turned to find a pudgy kid sitting in the passenger seat of the Incredibile.

"Who are you?" Mr. Incredible asked.

"I'm Incrediboy!" the kid answered enthusiastically.

"What? No . . . ," Mr. Incredible said as he looked him over. The redheaded kid was wearing a mask and a homemade Super suit. Then Mr. Incredible recognized him.

"Buddy?" he asked.

Buddy, the president of the Mr. Incredible Fan Club, answered with a frown. "My name is INCREDIBOY!"

"Look," Mr. Incredible said, trying to be patient, "I've stood for every photo, signed every scrap of paper, but this is a bit much."

But Buddy wasn't listening. "You don't have to worry about training me," he answered quickly. "I know all your moves—your crime-fighting style, everything!" The volume of Buddy's voice suddenly cranked up to ten. "I'm your number-one fan!" he yelled.

Suddenly, the door of the Incredibile whooshed open, ejecting an angry Incrediboy onto the side of the road.

Mr. Incredible hit the afterburners and peeled out.

Chapter 2

The bus robber was hiding on a rooftop, rooting through a stolen purse. The crook never saw Mr. Incredible's shadow looming over him.

"You can tell a lot about a woman by the contents of her purse. But maybe that's not what you had in mind," Mr. Incredible said. The crook pulled a gun and backed away from the formidable hero. *Whack!* A punch seemed to come from nowhere, dropping the thief.

But the punch hadn't come from Mr. Incredible.

Mr. Incredible looked over his shoulder. Then he smiled. A dazzling masked woman smiled back.

"Elastigirl," he said knowingly.

"Mr. Incredible," she replied as she stretched out an arm to lift the thug to his feet.

"It's all right," he told her. "I've got him."

"Sure you've got him," she said, snapping her arm back. "I just took him out for you."

The two heroes stepped back and playfully argued about who would take the bus robber in.

"We could share, you know," she said, stretching

toward him with graceful ease.

"I work alone," Mr. Incredible said coolly.

"Well," Elastigirl said, looping herself around him in one fluid motion, "I think you need to be more . . . flexible."

"You doing anything later?" Mr. Incredible asked, raising an eyebrow.

"I have a previous engagement," she whispered pointedly as she stretched across the rooftops and disappeared.

Mr. Incredible watched in admiration as the beautiful Super woman left. Then he turned his attention back to the bus robber and handcuffed him.

The crack of gunfire filled the air as a black helicopter armed to the teeth buzzed the rooftops, zooming away from something—or someone.

Mr. Incredible looked up. "Frozone," he said with a smile.

Frozone swooped down, traveling on sheets of ice he threw from rooftop to rooftop. A fellow Super, Frozone could create ice from the moisture in the air. Ice bolts shot from his palm as he chased the fleeing helicopter.

Frozone noticed Mr. Incredible as he passed. "Shouldn't you be getting ready?" he shouted.

Mr. Incredible yelled back. "Hey . . . I've still got time!"

The sound of a woman's scream caught Mr. Incredible's attention. He turned to see someone pointing to the top of a giant skyscraper. A man on a ledge was about to jump. A crowd was quickly forming in the street.

The crowd gasped as the man stepped off the ledge and tumbled toward the pavement.

Mr. Incredible burst into action with a calculated jump from the roof of a lower building. He tackled the jumper in midair and sailed across the street, crashing through a window. In a shower of glass, they landed in the empty lobby of a bank.

"I think you broke something," the jumper moaned.

"With counseling, I think you'll come to forgive me," Mr. Incredible told him. Then his crime sense kicked in. Something was wrong.

He was taking a look around the bank when suddenly there was a booming explosion. A huge safe door flew through the air and landed on Mr. Incredible, pinning him to the ground. Out of the smoke and rubble stepped Bomb Voyage, a super villain from France. It seemed Mr. Incredible had stumbled into a bank robbery in progress.

Mr. Incredible rolled the safe door aside. "Bomb Voyage!" He stepped forward to stop the villain.

"Monsieur Incroyable," replied the notorious thief.

"And Incrediboy!" said a voice from behind Mr. Incredible.

"Incrediboy?" Bomb Voyage mocked.

Buddy was back. Flashing his homemade rocket boots, he asked Mr. Incredible, "Aren't you curious how I get around so fast?"

"Go home, Buddy," Mr. Incredible told him.

"This is because I don't have powers, isn't it?" Buddy said angrily. "You can be Super without them. I invented these." Buddy lifted one of his rocket boots so Mr. Incredible could get a better look. "I can fly! Can *you* fly?"

"Fly home, Buddy," Mr. Incredible told him. "I work alone."

"I'll show you," Buddy insisted. "I'll go get the police!"

But Bomb Voyage wasn't about to let either of them ruin his day. As Buddy dashed for the shattered window, Bomb Voyage secretly clipped a small bomb to Buddy's cape.

Mr. Incredible spotted the bomb. He raced after

Buddy and grabbed the cape, yelling, "Buddy, don't!" But it was too late. Buddy jumped, activating his rocket boots in a shower of sparks and lifting Mr. Incredible into the air with him.

Mr. Incredible fought to get hold of the bomb as he and Buddy streaked across the sky.

"Let go!" Buddy shouted. "You're wrecking my flight pattern!"

Mr. Incredible reached the bomb and tore it from Buddy's cape. The bomb fell, as did Mr. Incredible. Both landed on the tracks of an elevated train. The bomb exploded. The blast ripped through a huge section of track just as a train was approaching. Mr. Incredible had to stop the train before it came to the missing tracks!

Using his Super strength, Mr. Incredible held his body up against the oncoming train. *Screeeeeeeee!* The sound of screeching metal filled the air as Mr. Incredible used every ounce of his Super strength to halt the train.

Chapter 3

Thanks to Mr. Incredible, the train was stopped and no one was seriously hurt. Mr. Incredible had Buddy by the back of the neck. "Take this one home," he said to a police officer, "and make sure his mom knows what he's been doing."

"You're making a mistake," Buddy protested. "I could help you!"

Mr. Incredible told the police about the injured jumper and the bank robbery. "The blast in that building was caused by Bomb Voyage. We might be able to nab him if we set up a perimeter."

"You mean he got away?" an officer asked.

"Well, yeah," Mr. Incredible answered, nodding at Buddy. "Skippy here made sure of that."

"Incrediboy!" Buddy said again.

Mr. Incredible turned to Buddy. "You're not affiliated with me!"

A tiny alarm sounded. Mr. Incredible checked his watch. "Holy smokes! I'm late!" he said. "Listen, I have to be somewhere." He signaled the Incredibile, and the futuristic vehicle came roaring around the corner and up to its owner.

"But what about Bomb Voyage?" asked one of the officers.

"Any other night I'd go after him myself," Mr. Incredible answered as he climbed into the car. "But I've really gotta go. Don't worry, we'll get him eventually!"

Mr. Incredible fired the afterburners and sped off.

"You're very late," Frozone said flatly. Mr. Incredible fumbled with his bow tie. "How do I look?" he asked.

"The mask!" Frozone said, stopping him. "You've still got the mask on!"

Frozone pulled the mask off Mr. Incredible. Mr. Incredible took a deep breath and pushed open the chapel doors. Smartly dressed in a black tuxedo again, he took a step down the aisle of the large cathedral.

Frozone, his best man, followed him.

They walked to the altar, where Mr. Incredible's beautiful bride was waiting. The ceremony began. "Robert Parr, will you have this woman to be your lawfully wedded wife?"

His wife-to-be, Elastigirl, also known as

Helen, whispered, "Cutting it kind of close, don't you think?"

Mr. Incredible smiled. "You need to be more . . . flexible," he replied with a wink.

The ceremony concluded: "As long as you both shall live?"

"I do," answered Mr. Incredible, taking Elastigirl in his arms. The crowd of Supers in the cathedral stood up and cheered.

"As long as we both shall live," Elastigirl promised. "No matter what happens."

"We're Supers," Mr. Incredible said confidently. "What could happen?"

"This flash from the news desk: In a stunning turn of events, a Super is being sued for saving someone who, apparently, did not want to be saved. The plaintiff, who was foiled in his attempted suicide by Mr. Incredible, has filed a suit against the famed hero in Superior Court."

On the crowded steps of the courthouse, a lawyer spoke to the media. "My client didn't ask to be saved. He didn't want to be saved," he said dryly.

A masked Mr. Incredible appeared on the courthouse steps in a blue business suit and tie.

"I saved your life!" he said, pointing at his accuser.

"You ruined my death!" the man shouted back.

Five days later, the injured victims of the train accident also filed a suit. Mr. Incredible's court losses cost the government millions.

Suddenly, it seemed to be open season on Supers everywhere. The newspapers were filled with headlines accusing the Supers of harming, not helping, people. The lawsuits began to pile up.

Even the government turned against them. "It is time for their secret identities to become their *only* identities," one congresswoman demanded. "Time for them to join us, or go away."

There was some protest in favor of the Supers, but finally, under tremendous pressure and a mountain of lawsuits, the government quietly initiated the Super Relocation Program (otherwise known as the SRP). Supers promised never to use their Super powers again, in exchange for anonymity.

The Supers found themselves with new names and identities. From now on, they would live average lives, quietly blending in with the rest of society.

And just like that, the golden age of Supers was over.

Chapter 4

Fifteen years later, Mr. Incredible, now known as Bob Parr, sat in his small cubicle at the Insuricare insurance company, stamping the word DENIED in red ink on everything that passed his desk. His white collar was a bit too tight, his uncomfortable chair a bit too small. Bob Parr, an insurance adjuster, was sixty-four pounds overweight and losing his hair. It was hard to believe he was the man the world had once known as Mr. Incredible.

A frail elderly woman sat in Bob's cubicle. She held in her hand a piece of paper stamped with red ink.

"Denied?" asked old Mrs. Hogenson, confused and upset. "You're denying my claim?"

"I'm sorry, Mrs. Hogenson," Bob told her, "but our liability is spelled out in paragraph seventeen." He was about to explain when the phone interrupted him. It was Helen.

She held the phone in the crook of her neck as she tried to get baby Jack-Jack out of the bath. The mask she had once worn as Elastigirl was gone; her shiny red thigh-high boots had been replaced by a pair of sensible shoes.

"I'm calling to celebrate a momentous occasion!" she said as Jack-Jack squirmed. "We are now officially moved in. I finally unpacked the last box!" The Parrs had moved a number of times since they'd entered the SRP. Helen had high hopes that this move would stick.

"That's great, honey," Bob answered, "but I have a client here. . . ."

"Say no more," Helen said brightly. "Go save the world one policy at a time. I've gotta go pick up the kids from school. See you tonight."

"Bye, honey," Bob said into the phone, and then looked at the sad face of Mrs. Hogenson. "Excuse me, where were we?"

Mrs. Hogenson explained that she desperately needed the money from her insurance policy. "If you can't help me, I don't know what I'll do," she said quietly.

Bob thought for a minute, checked to make sure that the coast was clear outside his cubicle, and then quickly whispered to Mrs. Hogenson every possible loophole she could use to get Insuricare to pay her claim.

"Oh, thank you," Mrs. Hogenson said gratefully.

Bob gave her a little smile and then told her to pretend to be upset just in case anyone was eavesdropping.

"I'm sorry, ma'am, but there's nothing I can do," Bob said, loudly enough for people to hear him. Mrs. Hogenson patted Bob's hand and left the office.

Bob's boss, Gilbert Huph, a small and mean-spirited man, suddenly barged into Bob's cubicle.

"Parr!" he yelled. "You authorized payment on the Walker policy?"

"Their policy clearly covers them against—" Bob began.

"I don't want to know about their coverage! Tell me how you're keeping Insuricare in the black." Huph continued angrily. "Tell me how that is possible with you writing checks to every Harry Hardluck and Sally Sobstory that gives you a call."

Huph stormed off, leaving Bob mute—a typical day at the office.

Chapter 5

Helen Parr had been hoping to pile the kids into her station wagon and get home in time to make dinner. Instead, she was heading to the principal's office. Dash, the Parrs' older son, was in trouble again.

Dash had been born with the Super power of lightning-fast speed. But of course, since Supers weren't supposed to be Super, he was never allowed to use it, and the Parr family *had* to keep it a secret.

"What's this about? Has Dash done something wrong?" Helen asked the school principal when she got to the office, where Dash was waiting.

"He put thumbtacks on my stool!" Dash's fourth-grade teacher, Bernie Kropp, told Helen. "And this time I've got him!" Mr. Kropp continued triumphantly. "I hid a camera!"

He dropped a disc into a player. Helen and Dash held their breath and stared at the TV screen. There was Mr. Kropp, about to sit in his chair. He sat . . . and screamed. No sign of Dash at all. *"See?"*

Mr. Kropp shouted, replaying it.

The school principal looked at Mr. Kropp. The teacher sounded completely nuts. Helen breathed a sigh of relief.

"Bernie . . . ," the principal said.

"Don't 'Bernie' me!" Mr. Kropp protested. "This little rat is guilty!"

The principal turned to Helen. "You and your son can go now, Mrs. Parr. I'm sorry for the trouble."

As Helen hurried Dash out the door, she could hear Bernie Kropp yelling, "You're letting him go *again*? He's guilty! You can see it on his smug little face! Guilty! Guilty! Guilty!"

"Dash!" Helen exclaimed when she got him into the car. "This is the third time this year you've been sent to the office! We need to find a better outlet."

Dash slumped in his seat. "Maybe I could, if you'd let me go out for sports," he muttered glumly.

"Honey," Helen answered. "You know why we can't do that."

"But I promise I'll slow up!" Dash offered. "I'll only be the best by a tiny bit."

But Helen knew the world didn't want them to

be their best, not even by a little bit.

She shook her head. "Right now, honey, the world just wants us to fit in."

"But Dad always says our powers are nothing to be ashamed of. Our powers made us special."

"Everyone's special," Helen sighed wearily.

"Which is another way of saying no one is," Dash said, sulking.

Helen drove the station wagon to the junior high to pick up Dash's older sister, Violet. Helen looked around. Violet was nowhere to be seen—but then, that was one of her talents. Violet had the power to turn invisible. This came in handy when she felt shy around boys, especially Tony Rydinger.

Violet also had the power of generating force fields, but that was only good for fights with Dash. He hated it when she used her force fields.

Violet was invisible now, as she peeked over the top of a bush and watched Tony Rydinger come down the school steps. He stopped for a second and then looked over his shoulder. Seeing nothing, he walked away. Violet shyly rematerialized and blushed. Then she scampered into her mother's car.

Chapter 6

It was dinnertime at the Parr home.

"Do you have to read at the table?" Helen asked Bob as she quickly used a spoon to scoop up dribbling baby food from Jack-Jack's face.

Bob, who was reading his newspaper, didn't hear the question. He was lost in the news.

"Uh-huh, yeah," he said distractedly.

Helen sighed and turned to Dash. "Smaller bites, Dash," she suggested. But Dash didn't seem to hear her either. "Bob, could you help the carnivore cut his meat?"

Bob sighed, put down his paper, and reached over to Dash's plate with a fork and knife.

"You have something you want to tell your father about school?" Helen asked Dash.

"Uh . . . we dissected a frog . . . ?" Dash asked, hoping to divert his mother's line of questioning.

Helen raised her eyebrows. "Dash got sent to the office again," she said matter-of-factly.

"Good . . . good," Bob answered, still reading the paper out of the corner of his eye as he cut the meat on Dash's plate.

"No, Bob. That's bad."

"What?" Bob said, finally looking up.

"Dash got sent to the office again," Helen repeated.

"What for?" asked Bob.

"Nothing," Dash said quickly.

"He put thumbtacks on his teacher's chair *during class,*" Helen said.

"Nobody saw me," Dash argued as Bob continued cutting. "You could barely see it on the tape!"

"They caught you on tape and you still got away with it?" Bob said with some pride. "Whoa! You must have been booking!"

"Bob!" Helen said. "We're not encouraging this."

"I'm not encouraging," Bob said, trying to hide his excitement. "I'm just asking how fast—" A sudden *crack* interrupted the conversation. Bob stopped cutting Dash's meat and looked down. Inadvertently using his Super strength, he had cut through the plate, and the dining room table, too.

"I'm getting a new plate," Bob said, and headed for the kitchen.

Helen turned to Violet, who was poking at her

dinner, her long hair covering most of her face. "How about you, Vi? How was school?"

Violet shrugged. "Nothing to report."

"You've hardly touched your food," Helen said.

"I'm not hungry for meat loaf," Violet answered.

Helen offered to get Vi something else. "What are you hungry for?"

"Tony Rydinger!" Dash teased.

"Shut up!" Vi said to him.

"Well, you are!" Dash laughed.

"I said shut up, you little insect!"

"Do *not* shout at the table!" Helen said firmly, and called Bob, who was still in the kitchen. "Honey!"

"She'd eat if we were having Tony loaf!" Dash giggled.

"That's it!" Vi shouted in frustration, lunging at Dash and then vanishing. Dash wrestled free and ran around the table in a blur. Jack-Jack giggled happily. Violet stopped Dash with her force field as Helen stretched her arms in all directions, trying to catch them. They dove under the table, continuing to wrestle.

In the kitchen, Bob was fixated on the newspaper. Under the headline PALADINO MISSING,

Bob read, "Simon J. Paladino, long an outspoken advocate of Supers' rights, is missing." Bob couldn't help wondering what had happened. Simon Paladino was the secret identity of Gazerbeam, a former Super and one of Bob's friends.

Then he heard Helen. "Bob?" she was calling desperately. "It's time to engage! Do something!"

Bob snapped out of it and entered the dining room. He hoisted the dinner table and his family over his head. Helen hung over the table as Dash and Vi dangled from her stretched arms. They were still fighting, twisting Helen's arms into a hopelessly tangled knot. Jack-Jack, loving the excitement, shrieked with joy.

Then the doorbell rang.

Everyone froze. Bob lowered the table, and the family resumed a "normal" dining position. Dash calmly stood up and answered the door.

"Hey, Speedo! Hey, Helen!" said a voice in the doorway. Everyone in the Parr house relaxed. It was Lucius Best, formerly known as Frozone!

"Hey!" shouted Bob warmly. "*Ice* of you to drop by!"

"Ha!" answered Lucius. "I never heard that one before."

Lucius Best, the guy who wrote the book on "cool," hadn't changed much since the old days. Sure, he had to hide the chilling Super powers he had used when he was known to the world as Frozone, but as with everything else, he was cool with that.

Bob ran to the hall closet and quickly grabbed his coat and bowling bag. "I'll be back later," he said to Helen.

Helen seemed confused.

"It's Wednesday," Bob reminded her.

Helen shook her head, remembering. "Oh . . . !" she said. "Bowling night."

She looked back at Dash and Vi, who were still ready to go at it, and then sighed.

"Say hello to Honey for me," Helen said to Lucius as he and Bob headed out the door.

"Will do," Lucius answered. "Good night, Helen. G'night, kids!"

Helen turned back to Dash. He wasn't going to get out of discussing his trip to the principal's office.

"I'm not the only kid who's been sent to the office, ya know," Dash said.

"Other kids don't have Super powers," Helen said, trying to be patient. "You were almost caught.

Now, it's perfectly normal for you to feel—"

"What does anyone in our family know about being normal?" Vi interrupted. "The only normal one is Jack-Jack."

Jack-Jack, the only member of the Parr family who didn't seem to have any Super powers, gleefully spit a mouthful of baby food onto his chin and giggled.

Chapter 7

Lucius drove to a run-down part of the city and parked in an alleyway. He and Bob weren't really going bowling. Instead, they sat in the car and reminisced about the old days while a portable police scanner hissed dispatch calls.

"So now I'm in deep trouble." Lucius laughed, telling Bob a story from his past. "I mean, one more jolt of this death ray and I'm an epitaph. So what does Baron Von Worthless do?"

"He starts monologuing!" Bob cracked up.

"He starts monologuing! He starts this, like, prepared speech about how feeble I am compared to him, how inevitable my defeat is, how the world will soon be his, yadda yadda yadda."

"Yammerin'!" Bob said, loving the story.

"Yammerin'," Lucius said even more loudly. "I mean, the guy has me on a platter and he won't shut up!"

A call suddenly crackled over the scanner: "Twenty-three fifty-six in progress."

"Twenty-three fifty-six," Bob repeated. "What is

that . . . robbery? Wanna catch a robber?"

"Tell you the truth," Lucius answered, "I'd rather go bowling. What if we actually did what our wives think we're doing for a change?"

As the former Supers continued to talk, they didn't even realize they were being watched. A beautiful blonde in a black sports car spoke into a headset.

"He's not alone," she said. "The fat guy's still with him."

The words "Fire at Fourth and Elias" came across Lucius's scanner. Bob lit up like a bulb.

"A fire! Yeah, baby!" Bob said, pulling on a ski mask. Lucius did the same, turned on the car, and headed in the direction of Fourth and Elias.

"We're gonna get caught," Lucius said.

As they tore down the street, the black sports car followed them.

Bob and Lucius could see the orange glow of the burning apartment building from a block away. They were the first to arrive at the scene. Together, they ran into the burning building, found the unconscious apartment dwellers, and stacked them on their shoulders.

"Is that everybody?" Lucius shouted to Bob.

"It should be," Bob answered through the thick smoke, trying to make his way back into the street. "Can't you put this out?"

Lucius tried to ice the flames. "I can't lay down a layer thick enough!" he said. "It's evaporating too fast!"

"What does that mean?" shouted Bob.

"It means it's hot and I'm dehydrated, Bob!"

"What?" yelled Bob. "You're out of ice? I thought you could use the water in the air!"

"There is no water in this air! What's your excuse? Run out of muscles?"

Then the two heard an incredible roar. They looked up. The flaming roof was about to collapse and trap them inside. Lucius shook his head and looked at Bob. "I wanted to go bowling!" he said, scowling.

A large chunk of the ceiling suddenly smashed to the floor in a burning heap. Bob looked around and spotted a way out. He shifted his stack of unconscious victims to one shoulder and looked at Lucius.

"All right," Bob shouted, taking charge. "Stay right on my tail, this is going to get hot!"

Bob suddenly ran full speed down the flaming

hallway. Lucius was right behind him. As they ran through the flames, Bob focused on the brick wall ahead. He picked up speed, gave a huge yell, and lowered his free shoulder into it. The heroes and their rescued fire victims smashed through the brick wall just as the burning building collapsed behind them.

Saved! Bob thought for an instant. Then an alarm went off. Bob and Lucius looked around. They had smashed through the wall of a jewelry store.

A rookie police officer who had responded to the fire alarm suddenly spied the two ski-masked men and drew his pistol. "Freeze!" he shouted.

Lucius noticed a watercooler and managed to convince the rookie officer that he needed a cup of water. Lucius slowly brought the cup of water to his mouth and smiled.

"Okay, you had your drink now," said the rookie officer.

"I know," replied Lucius. "Freeze."

A frigid blast split the air.

On the street, firefighters tended to the fire. Several more police officers had arrived. They heard a gunshot. Drawing their guns, the officers entered the jewelry store. But once inside, they stopped and looked at each other, bewildered. In front of them was a heap of rescued fire victims at the base of an enormous hole in the wall. Standing nearby was the rookie, stunned and blinking under a layer of ice. The bullet and its vapor trail were frozen in midair in front of them.

Bob and Lucius jumped back into their car and pulled off their ski masks.

"That was way too close," Lucius said, hitting the gas. "We're not doing that again."

As the taillights of Lucius's car sped away, the cool blonde in the black sports car radioed in to her headquarters. "Verify you want to switch targets? Over," the voice on the radio said.

"Trust me," she answered. "This is the one he's been waiting for."

Chapter 8

Bob tiptoed through the kitchen. He had grabbed the last chunk of chocolate cake from a plate on the counter and was quietly making his way into the living room when the lights suddenly snapped on. It was Helen. She was sitting in a living room chair in her bathrobe.

"You said you'd be back by eleven," she said.

"I said I'd be back later," Bob answered.

"I assumed you'd be back later," Helen said, peeved. "If you came back at all you'd be back later."

Helen's arm stretched to Bob's shoulder and pulled a piece of concrete off his coat. "Is this . . . rubble?" she asked him accusingly.

"It was just a little workout," Bob replied. "Just to stay loose."

Helen closed her eyes. "You know how I feel about that, Bob! We can't blow our cover again!"

Bob looked down at his singed coat. "The building was coming down anyway," he said, trying to explain.

"You knocked down a building?"

"It was on fire!" Bob argued. "Structurally unsound! I performed a public service. You act like that's a bad thing."

"It is a bad thing, Bob. Uprooting our family again so you can relive the glory days is a very bad thing!"

Some loose papers on the coffee table suddenly rustled as a breeze came through the room.

Bob sighed. "All right, Dash. I know you're listening. Come on out."

"Vi, you too, young lady," Helen added.

Dash moved out from behind a door as Violet rematerialized from behind the couch.

"It's okay, kids," Bob said gently. "We're just having a discussion."

"Pretty loud discussion," Violet said.

"But that's okay," Bob told them, trying to sound upbeat. "What's important is that Mommy and I are always a team, always united . . . against . . . uh . . ." Bob wasn't sure where he was going with this. "The forces of . . ."

"Pigheadedness?" Helen suggested.

Bob hesitated. "I was going to say 'evil' or something."

Helen stood up and stretched her arms around the kids' shoulders. "We're sorry we woke you," she told them. "Everything's okay. We should all be in bed."

Chapter 9

The next day, Bob was back at his tiny desk in his tiny cubicle at Insuricare. His intercom suddenly beeped. Bob hit the answer button.

"Mr. Huph would like to talk to you in his office," a voice said flatly.

"Now?" Bob asked.

"Now," the voice replied.

Bob rolled his eyes, got up, and walked from his windowless cubicle to Huph's office. He didn't notice the mysterious attractive blonde who slipped into his cubicle as he left.

Huph's office was larger than Bob's cubicle, but painfully tidy and completely joyless—a lot like Huph himself.

"Sit down," Huph told Bob.

Bob took a seat as Huph stood up at his desk. This put Bob at about eye level with the little man.

"I am not happy, Bob," Huph announced. "Not happy. Ask me why, Bob."

Bob blinked slowly. "Okay . . . why?"

"Why what? Be specific, Bob," Huph said,

crossing his arms and glaring at Bob.

Bob knew a visit to Huph's office always required patience. Suddenly, he noticed something going on outside Huph's window. A stocky man was suspiciously hanging around the back alley.

Keeping an eye on the guy in the alley, Bob answered, "Why are you unhappy?"

"Your customers make me unhappy, Bob."

"You've had complaints?" Bob asked.

"Complaints I can handle," Huph answered. "What I can't handle is your customers' inexplicable knowledge of Insuricare's inner workings. They're experts. Experts, Bob! Exploiting every loophole, dodging every obstacle! They're penetrating the bureaucracy!"

"Did I do something illegal?" Bob asked him calmly.

"No," said Huph, irritated.

"Are you saying we shouldn't help our customers?"

Huph gritted his teeth. "The law requires that I answer no."

"We're supposed to help people," Bob said.

"We're supposed to help *our* people!" Huph exploded. "Starting with our stockholders."

"You know, Bob," Huph went on, taking a breath and composing himself, "a company is like—"

"An enormous clock," Bob said dully, finishing the sentence for him. Bob had heard Huph's "enormous clock" lecture before.

Huph droned on about cogs and wheels: ". . . cogs that fit, Bob. Cooperative cogs." But Bob's attention was on the thug outside the window, who was now mugging a citizen. Every muscle in Bob's body tensed for action.

"You know what I mean by cooperative cogs?" Huph asked, meshing his fingers together. "Bob? Bob! Look at me when I'm talking to you, Parr!"

"That man out there!" Bob said, his eyes on the victim. "He needs help. He's getting mugged."

"Well, let's hope we don't cover him!" Huph said coldly as Bob suddenly stood and bolted for the door.

"I'll be right back," Bob said.

"Stop right now or you're fired!" Huph threatened.

Bob hesitated. He thought about Helen and the kids. Huph narrowed his eyes, sensing he had the advantage. Confidently, Huph said, "Close the door."

Bob slowly let go of the doorknob that he had

crushed in his powerful hand.

"Get over here, Bob," Huph told him.

Bob turned to face Huph. Through Huph's window, he could see the helpless crime victim lying on the street. The mugger had gotten away. Bob could feel his blood pressure rise. Suddenly, his enormous right hand flashed out and clamped around Huph's scrawny neck. Huph let out a tiny squeak.

The office staff watched as Huph crashed through four office walls before he slammed into a file cabinet, sending documents everywhere.

"Uh-oh," Bob mumbled.

Chapter 10

"How is he?" Bob asked.

"He'll live," replied Rick Dicker.

"I'm fired, aren't I?" asked Bob.

Rick Dicker, a government agent of the SRP, was a "tell it like it is" kind of guy, and he told Bob he was, indeed, fired. "We appreciate all you did in the old days," he said, "but from now on, Bob, you're on your own."

Bob nodded. He knew how complicated and expensive it was to relocate a Super once the Super's cover had been blown. Rick had done it for Bob more than a few times.

Dicker was in the hospital elevator when he said, "Listen. Maybe I could relocate you, for old times' sake."

Bob smiled and shook his head. "I can't do that to my family again. We just got settled. I'll make it work. Thanks," he said, and headed home.

Bob pulled into his driveway. A neighborhood kid on a trike was staring at him. "What are you waiting for?" Bob asked, getting out of his car.

"I dunno," the kid answered, looking around. He had once spied Bob lifting his car with one hand. "Something amazing, I guess."

A smile flashed over Bob's face and then faded. "Me too, kid. Me too."

Bob walked into the house. Helen was in the kitchen fixing dinner. He headed down to his den. It was the one place where he could proudly display his mementos of the old days.

They were all there: the amazing photos, the front-page headlines, the countless magazines, thank-you letters, and all his other triumphs. But the centerpiece hung on the wall, mounted behind a sheet of glass. It was his old blue and black Mr. Incredible suit. Seeing it today was almost more than Bob could take.

Bob set his briefcase on his desk, opened it, took out his Insuricare employee manual, and tossed it and everything else in his briefcase into the trash. But something hit the bottom of the trashcan with a clunk. Bob looked. It was a large manila envelope.

Bob picked it up and tore it open. Inside was a flat metal panel with a small circle in its center. Bob tried to read the tiny words inside the circle. He squinted and read, "'Hold still,'" out loud.

Suddenly, the panel projected a blue laser grid over Bob's face. A robotic voice began to speak. "Match. Mr. Incredible."

Bob jumped and dropped the panel onto his desk. A small rod rose from the panel and scanned the den. "Room is secure," the voice said. "Commence message."

The panel turned into a video screen. On it was the beautiful blonde from the black sports car. Bob was stunned. "Hello, Mr. Incredible," she said warmly. "Yes, we know who you are. Rest assured, your secret is safe with us. My name is Mirage. We have something in common. According to the government, neither of us exist. . . ."

Bob moved closer to the screen, mesmerized. "I represent a top-secret division of the government designing and testing experimental technology, and"— she paused—"we have need of your unique abilities."

"Honey?"

Bob jumped. It was Helen calling from the kitchen. "Dinner's ready!"

Bob turned back to the screen as Mirage continued. "Something has happened at our remote testing facility. A highly experimental prototype robot has escaped our control—"

"Honey!"

"Okay! Okay!" Bob shouted to Helen.

"It threatens to cause incalculable damage to itself and our testing facilities," Mirage said.

"Is someone in there?" Helen shouted.

"It's the TV! I'm trying to watch!" Bob yelled back. He put his face closer to the screen. He grabbed a pencil. He didn't want to miss any of this message.

"Because of its highly sensitive nature, this mission does not, nor will it ever, exist."

"Well, stop trying!" Helen said. "It's time for dinner!"

"One minute!" Bob yelled.

"If you accept, your payment will be triple your current annual salary." Bob's jaw dropped, and he blankly scribbled "BIG $$$$" on a pad.

"Call the number on the card," Mirage instructed as a business card spit out of the bottom of the video screen. "Voice matching will be used to ensure security. The Supers aren't gone, Mr. Incredible. You can still do great things. You have twenty-four hours to respond," she said smoothly. "Think about it."

Bob finished scribbling. His mind was reeling. Then the robotic voice came on again. "This message will self-destruct," it said.

From outside Bob's den, the family could hear a muffled boom!

From inside his den, Bob could hear the family suddenly scream as the sprinklers over the dining room table went off.

Bob and Helen finished drying out the inside of the house. "You're one distracted guy," Helen said as she used a hair dryer on the kids' books.

"Hmm? Am I?" Bob said. "Don't mean to be."

Helen put her arm around him. "I know you miss being a hero and your job is frustrating. I just want you to know how much it means to me that you stay at it anyway."

"Honey," Bob said, looking away, "about the job . . ."

Helen was suddenly alarmed. "What?"

"Uh, I . . . uh," Bob stammered. "Something's happened."

"What?" Helen asked.

Bob gulped hard. "Uh, the company's sending me to a conference out of town," he said finally.

"I'm just gonna be gone for a few days."

"A conference? This is good, isn't it?" she said hopefully. "You see? They're finally recognizing your talents!" She gave him a hug.

"Yes," Bob said, hugging her back.

Bob went down to his den. He picked up the phone and dialed the number on the card. A female voice answered.

"This is Mr. Incredible," Bob said. "I'm in." He hung up the phone and glanced at his Mr. Incredible suit on the wall.

Chapter 11

Bob sat back in a sleek luxurious jet as it sliced through the sky. He was on his way to a remote secret location. Clad in his old Super suit, now a little tight around the middle, Bob faced the beautiful Mirage. She began briefing him on his upcoming mission.

"The Omnidroid 9000 is a top-secret prototype battle robot," she told Bob. "Its artificial intelligence enables it to solve any problem. And unfortunately—"

"Let me guess," Bob said. "It got smart enough to wonder why it had to take orders."

Mirage nodded. "We lost control and now it's loose in the jungle."

"How am I going in?" Bob asked in a cool tone.

"An airdrop from five thousand feet," Mirage said. It had been a long time since Bob had been air-dropped into anything. He played it cool, but secretly he couldn't wait.

"We're pretty sure it's on the southern half of the island," Mirage told Bob. "One more thing," she said.

"Obviously it represents a significant investment."

Bob understood. "You want me to shut it down without completely destroying it."

Mirage smiled. "You *are* Mr. Incredible."

Bob confidently entered the drop-pod bay. Getting into the pod proved a Super feat in itself. After a few unsuccessful attempts at squeezing himself in, he was finally crammed inside the pod. Admittedly, he wasn't in top Super form. Mirage entered the drop-pod bay and pressed the speaker switch.

"Remember," she said, "it's a learning robot. Every moment you spend fighting it only increases its knowledge of how to beat you."

Bob nodded and repeated his instructions. "Shut it down. Do it quickly. Don't destroy it," he said.

"And don't die," Mirage added. Bob flashed her a smile, and the pod blasted from the jet into the clouds above the island of Nomanisan.

The pod dropped and disappeared into the thick jungle. Bob had to tear the pod apart to get out. Freed, he quickly began to track the robot. Mr. Incredible was ready for action.

Unfortunately, he was also out of shape. By the time Mr. Incredible found the first sign of the

Omnidroid, he was breathing heavily. Then, crashing out of the jungle, the robot attacked him. Mr. Incredible, overweight and a little rusty, struggled with the large spiderlike robot. He hadn't fought like this in a long time. He managed to throw the robot into a nearby lava pool, but hurt his back in the process.

"Ow! My back!" he cried.

The robot emerged, red-hot from the lava, and grabbed him with two claws, trying to break him in half! Mr. Incredible's back cracked. He smiled. The Omnidroid was better than a chiropractor! With newfound strength he slipped under the robot and tore his way inside the machine. The Omnidroid began attacking itself to get at Mr. Incredible, eventually pulling itself apart in the process.

In a secret room in the island's headquarters, Mirage and her mysterious employer watched a video display of the battle.

"Surprising," the mystery man commented to Mirage as they watched Mr. Incredible. "We must bring him back." He smiled. "Invite him to dinner."

Later that evening, Bob, handsomely dressed in a tuxedo, opened the door to an enormous dining room.

No one was there. He glanced at his watch. He was early. The dining room had a terrace that overlooked a lush tropical jungle. The lavishly set table was placed in front of an impressive waterfall of molten lava.

Suddenly, there was a rumble. The hot lava parted like a curtain, revealing a passageway. Bob slipped out of the room and peeked through a crack in the door. He could see two figures behind the falls. He recognized one of them as Mirage. The other was obscured by the lava's glow. Bob closed the door. Mirage opened the door moments later to see Bob—seemingly just arriving at the room.

"Am I overdressed?" he asked as he stepped into the dining room.

Mirage smiled approvingly. "Actually, you look rather dashing."

They sat at the dining room table, the red lava falling behind them. "I take it our host is—" Bob began.

"I'm sorry. He's not able to dine with us tonight," Mirage said with a wave of her hand. "He hopes you'll understand."

"Of course," Bob said casually. "I do usually make it a point to know who I'm working for."

Mirage explained that their host preferred anonymity. "Surely you of all people understand that," she said, smiling.

Bob looked at the surroundings. "I was just wondering . . . of all places to settle down," he said, "why live—"

"With a volcano?" Mirage laughed. "He's attracted to power. So am I." She leaned toward Bob. "It's a weakness we share."

"Seems a bit unstable," Bob said.

"I prefer to think of it as misunderstood," Mirage said, looking at Bob over her raised glass.

Chapter 12

Bob returned home and felt like a new man. Over the next few weeks, he began working out, getting in shape again. He bought the brand-new sports car he'd always dreamed about for himself and a new car for Helen. For the first time in years, he felt *incredible.*

As he dressed the next morning in a tailored business suit, Bob noticed a tear in his Mr. Incredible suit.

"Hurry, honey, or you'll be late for work!" Helen called. Bob quickly stuffed his old Super suit into his briefcase and snapped it shut. He still hadn't told Helen he'd been fired from Insuricare. He'd been pretending to go to work every morning.

Helen hugged him at the doorstep. "Have a great day, honey! Help customers! Climb ladders!" she said, brightened by Bob's new attitude.

Bob waved from his new sports car, revved the engine a bit, and backed down the driveway.

An hour later, he pulled up to an enormous gate of webbed laser beams and leaned out his window toward the video security monitor.

The screen flashed on. "Do you have an appointment?" a guard asked stiffly.

"I'm an old friend," Bob answered. "I just wanted—"

"Get back, Rolf!" a husky voice suddenly barked over the speaker. "Go check the electric fence or something."

Bob couldn't see anyone on the screen but the guard. But a familiar face wearing huge dark-rimmed glasses rose into the bottom half of the screen. It was his old friend, internationally famous fashion designer Edna Mode.

"What is it?" she asked in her brusque but fabulous accent. "What do you want?"

Bob took off his sunglasses and grinned at the security camera.

Edna, known to her good friends simply as E, was stunned. "My God, you have gotten fat!" she said. "Come in! Come!"

The laser beams shut down. Bob drove through the gate and up the long driveway. E, now in her sixties, greeted Bob warmly as he entered her modern, gallery-like home. She reached up and took Bob's arm. She led him into her gigantic living room.

"Yes, things are going quite well, but"—she sighed—"you know, it is not the same. Not the same at all."

Bob nodded. "Weren't you just in the news?" he asked. "Some show in Prague?"

"Milan, darling, Milan. Supermodels—*Hah!* Nothing *Super* about them. *Feh!* I used to design for gods!" Then E looked at Bob hopefully. "But perhaps you come with a challenge, eh?"

Bob held up his suit. "E, I just need a patch job."

E grabbed the torn suit. "This is megamesh," she told him impatiently, "outmoded but very sturdy, and you have torn right through it."

She looked up. "What have you been doing, Robert? Moonlighting hero work?"

Bob tried to sound casual. "Must've happened a long time ago."

"Ah," E said knowingly. "I see."

E stood up. "This is a hobo suit," she announced firmly. "You cannot be seen in this. I won't allow it. Fifteen years ago, maybe. But now!" She shook her head and dropped the suit into the trash.

"What do you mean?" Bob asked, rushing to retrieve it. "You designed it."

"I never look back, darling," she said with a

wave of her hand. "It distracts me from the *now.* You need a new suit. That much is certain."

"A new suit?" Bob was shocked. "Where would I get—"

"Ask me now before I again become sane," E said. It was a hint.

"Wait," Bob said, confused. "You want to make me a suit?"

E suddenly began gesturing with her tiny arms. "It will be bold. Dramatic! Heroic!"

"Yeah!" Bob agreed enthusiastically. "Something classic, like Dynaguy. He had a great look. The cape and the boots—"

"No capes," said E, cutting him off.

"Isn't that my decision?" Bob asked.

E stiffened and reminded Bob of all the past caped Supers. "Do you remember Thunderhead?" she asked.

Bob cringed.

"Tall? Storm powers? Nice man," E said. "Good with kids. His cape snagged on a missile fin."

"Thunderhead was not the brightest bulb in the—!" Bob said, hoping to change her mind.

E raised an eyebrow and ran down the list of doomed Supers.

"Stratogale," she said. "Cape caught in a jet turbine."

Bob sighed.

"Metaman," E continued. "Express elevator. Dynaguy—snag on takeoff."

E glared at Bob. *"No capes!"* she said with a finality Bob wasn't about to argue with. Then she smiled. "Well, go on," she told him. "Your new suit will be finished before your next assignment."

"I only need a patch job, E," Bob said, looking at his old suit. "For sentimental reasons."

"Fine," E sighed, taking the suit from Bob. "I will also fix the hobo suit."

Bob smiled at his old friend. "E, you're the best of the best!"

E closed her eyes and smiled. "Yes, I know, darling. I know."

Chapter 13

Helen was home doing laundry. She was about to hang Bob's sports coat when she saw it: the glint of something shiny on his jacket—a long blond hair. The phone rang. Bob yelled that he'd get it and picked it up in the den. Helen slyly picked up the bedroom phone anyway.

She heard a woman's voice say, "How soon can you get here?"

"I'll leave tomorrow morning," Bob answered quickly, and then hung up the phone.

"Who was that, honey?" Helen asked as Bob came out of his den. "The office?"

Bob shrugged. "Another conference," he said. "Short notice, but duty calls." Bob smiled, but Helen was growing suspicious.

The next morning, Mr. Incredible found himself once again in the luxurious surroundings of the sleek jet. But this time, he was wearing his newly made and completely redesigned Super suit—dramatic, heroic, red—no cape. Mr. Incredible sipped his drink as the jet cut through the sky.

A voice came over the autopilot. "This is your automated captain speaking. Currently seventy-eight degrees in Nomanisan. Please fasten your seat belt. We're beginning our descent."

Mr. Incredible glanced out the jet's window as it began to drop. He could see the lush volcanic terrain of Nomanisan coming up fast.

Suddenly, Mr. Incredible heard the autopilot cut the engines. The jet plunged, nose down, into the sea. As it hit the surface, the jet converted into a high-speed submersible.

The jet-sub maneuvered through rock formations as it headed toward the island of Nomanisan. Mr. Incredible watched the spectacular underwater scenery as it passed his window.

Ahead, an underwater docking bay opened. The submersible passed through a blue curtain of bubbles created by the cooling lava, and settled to a landing. The water drained from around the ship. Mr. Incredible heard the clunk of a docking tube as it attached to a door.

"Hello, Mr. Incredible," Mirage said as the door opened. "Welcome back."

They stepped into a waiting monopod that

zoomed from the lagoon, through the jungle, and into the island headquarters.

Mirage escorted Mr. Incredible to his quarters and told him he'd be briefed in the conference room at two o'clock.

Chapter 14

Helen's day wasn't quite as exciting. She was tidying up Bob's den, dusting the glass case, when she noticed the case was open. She took a closer look and saw a long, nearly microscopic stitch in his old Super suit. Helen was shocked. It had been newly repaired.

"Edna," she said to herself. Helen knew that type of craftsmanship couldn't have been done by anyone else.

Helen decided that if Bob was doing Super work on the side, she wanted to know. There was only one thing to do. She picked up the phone and dialed a number she had never thought she would dial again.

"Hello," Helen said. "I'd like to speak to Edna, please."

"This is Edna," E replied.

"E, this is Helen."

"Helen who?" E asked in her usual husky voice.

"Uh, Helen Parr, er, uh . . . you know . . . Elastigirl."

E was thrilled. “Darling!” she said. “It’s been such a long time. So long!”

“Yes, it has been a while,” Helen said, hesitating. “Listen, there’s only one person Bob would trust to patch his Super suit, and that’s you, E.”

“Yes, yes, yes. Marvelous, isn’t it? Much better than those horrible pajamas he used to wear. They are all finished; when are you coming to see me? Do not make me beg, darling, I will not do it, you know!”

“Beg? Uh, no, I’m calling to beg about—I’m calling about Bob’s suit!” Helen said finally.

“You come in one hour, darling,” E said. “I insist. Okay? Okay. Bye.”

Chapter 15

Back in an enormous Nomanisan conference room, Mr. Incredible was waiting to be briefed on his next dangerous mission. He checked his watch. It was exactly two o'clock.

Two huge doors at the end of the conference room suddenly slammed open. But it wasn't Mirage. Another Omnidroid stood in the hangarlike doorway that opened to the jungle, but this one was not like the other Omnidroid.

"It's bigger!" a voice echoed over a loud-speaker as Mr. Incredible tried to maneuver around the robot. "It's badder!" the voice continued as the Omnidroid seemed to anticipate the Super's every move.

"It's too much for Mr. Incredible!" the voice boomed as the Omnidroid grabbed Mr. Incredible with a huge claw and flung him into a jungle clearing. It seized the Super in one of its giant claws as two spinning claws closed in on his neck. A chunky, wild-haired figure in a bright suit suddenly appeared.

"It's finally ready!" The caped stranger laughed.

"After you trashed the last one, I had to make some major modifications. Sure, it was difficult, but you're worth it. After all—I am your biggest fan."

A dark look of realization fell over Mr. Incredible's face. "Buddy?"

"My name is not Buddy!" he said, and pressed a button on his thick platinum wristband. The Omnidroid flung Mr. Incredible again. "And it's not Incrediboy either," Buddy went on. "That ship has sailed. All I wanted was to help you. I only wanted to help! And what did you say to me?"

Mr. Incredible remembered his words: *"Fly home, Buddy. I work alone."*

"I was wrong to treat you that way. I'm sorry," the Super said.

"See? Now you respect me. I'm a threat. That's the way it works. Turns out there are a lot of people, whole countries, who want respect. And they will pay through the nose to get it. How do you think I got rich? I invented weapons. Now I have a weapon that only I can defeat, and when I unleash it, I'll get everyone's respect. I am Syndrome!"

Mr. Incredible suddenly reached for a fallen log and hurled it at Syndrome with all his Super strength. Syndrome ducked and shot a beam from

As Bob Parr, Mr. Incredible misses being a real hero.

Bob remembers the good old days.

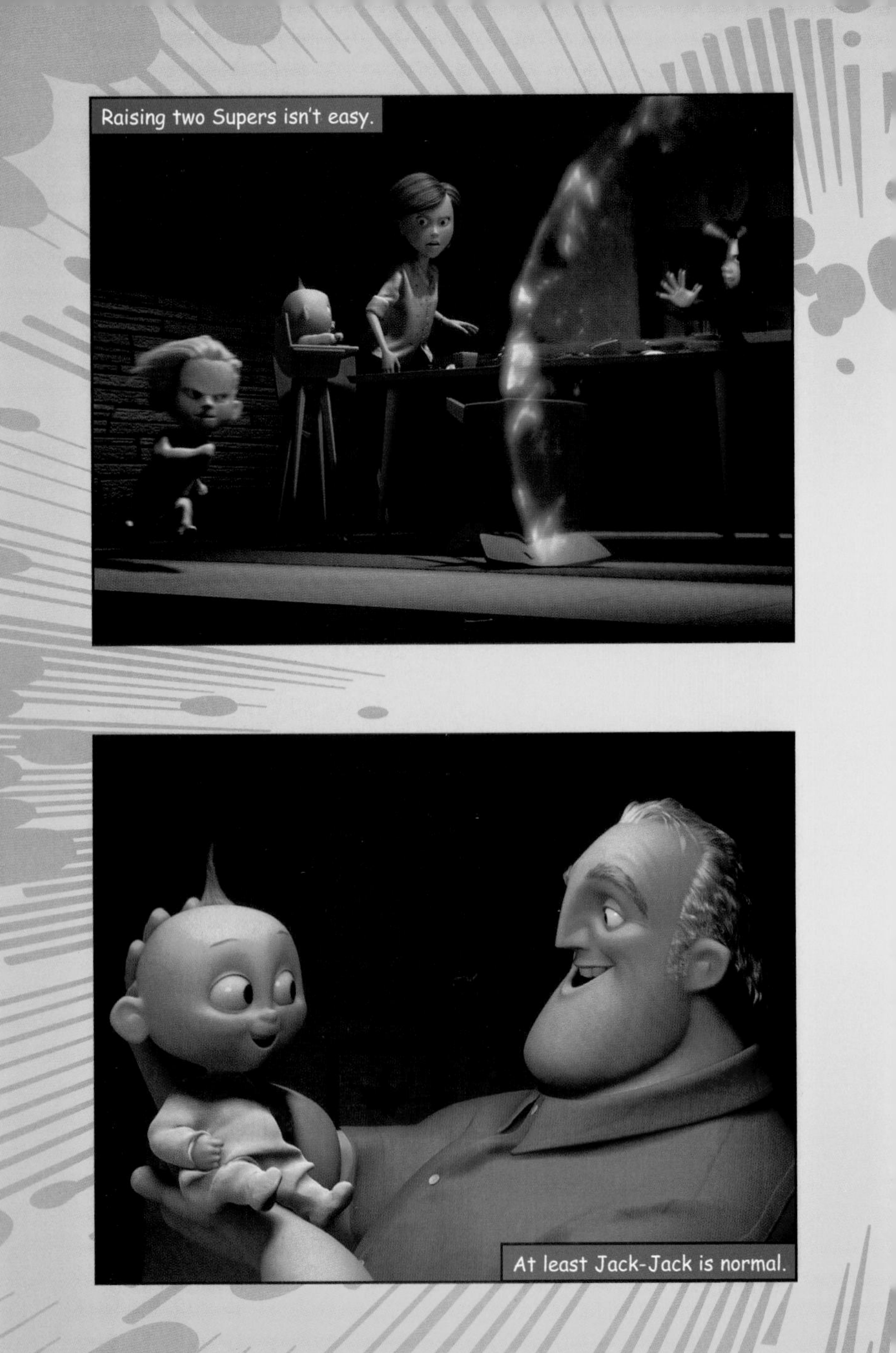
Raising two Supers isn't easy.
At least Jack-Jack is normal.

Mirage recruits Mr. Incredible for a top-secret assignment.

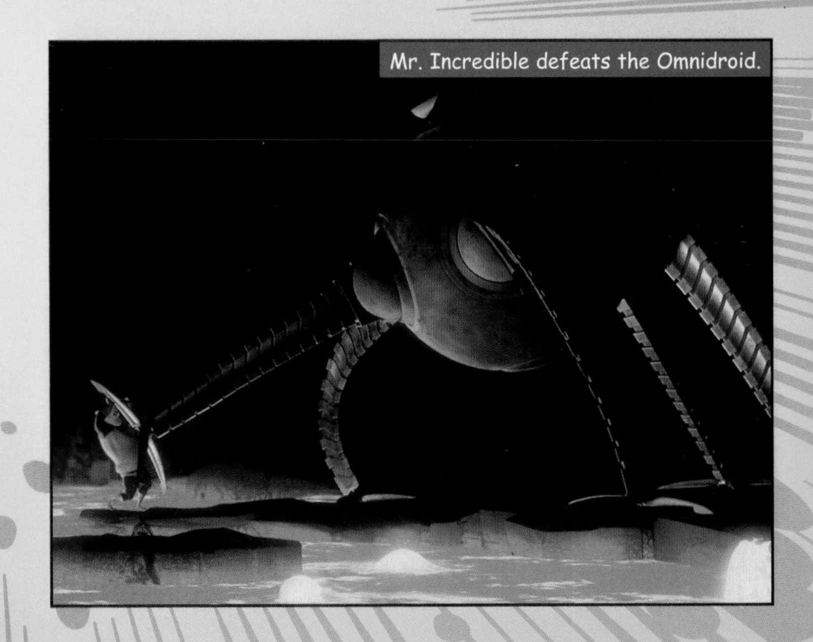

Mr. Incredible defeats the Omnidroid.

Bob starts getting into shape.
Edna decides to make a new
suit for Mr. Incredible.

Mr. Incredible is back for his next Super assignment.

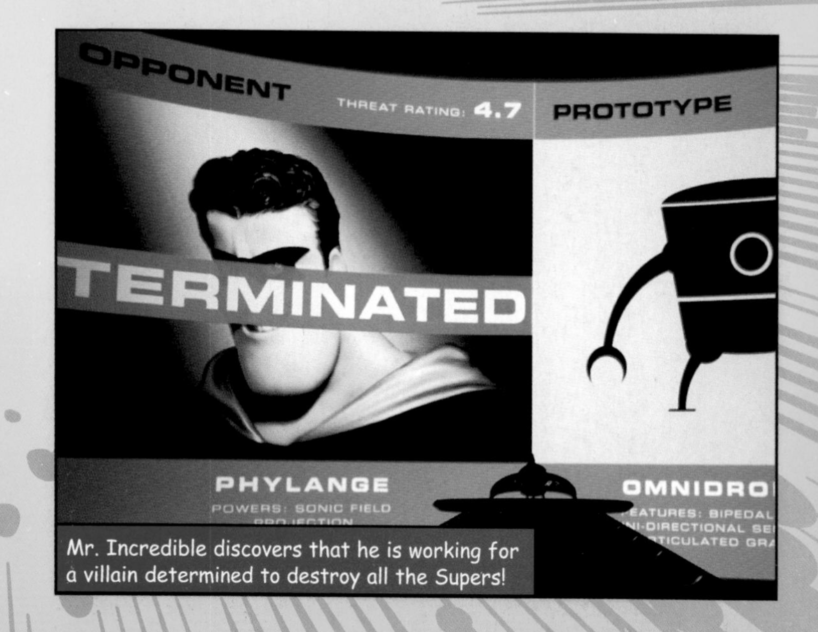
OPPONENT
THREAT RATING: 4.7
PROTOTYPE
TERMINATED
PHYLANGE
POWERS: SONIC FIELD
Mr. Incredible discovers that he is working for a villain determined to destroy all the Supers!

Syndrome taunts Mr. Incredible with his evil plan.

Elastigirl stretches to the rescue!

Dash and Vi use their powers to escape Syndrome's guards.
Mr. Incredible believes he has lost his family.

Together, the family battles Syndrome's guards.

Mr. Incredible and Frozone face the deadly Omnidroid.

his index finger, hitting the hero in the chest. Mr. Incredible froze in midair.

"You sly dog! You got me monologuing!" Syndrome chuckled with admiration. Then, jerking his index finger, he effortlessly tossed Mr. Incredible into a tree with tremendous force.

"Cool, huh? Zero-point energy. I save the best inventions for myself!"

With a slight move of his finger, Syndrome caught Mr. Incredible in his immobi-ray again, freezing him in midair. "Am I good enough now? Who's Super now?" Syndrome taunted as he slammed Mr. Incredible into the ground over and over.

"I'm Syndrome! Your nemesis! And . . ."

Syndrome suddenly caught himself monologuing again and realized he hadn't heard Mr. Incredible's body land. He flew over the jungle canopy to watch Mr. Incredible dive off a massive waterfall. Syndrome looked over a ledge as the Super crashed into the water below the falls. Furious, Syndrome engaged a small lollipop-shaped device from his wristband and dropped it into the water. It was a very powerful explosive.

The shock wave from the explosion blew Mr. Incredible through a cave into a grotto above the water. Exhausted, he was looking for a possible way out when he saw the skeleton of Gazerbeam. He recognized the glasses that hung on the old Super's skull. He remembered reading that Gazerbeam was missing, and shook his head sadly. But Mr. Incredible had to hand it to his old hero friend—in Gazerbeam's dying moments, he had used his laser eyes to burn the word *KRONOS* into the cave wall. Mr. Incredible knew it meant something important, but what?

Mr. Incredible heard the *click, click, click* of an electronic probe. It was entering the grotto. He quickly crawled under Gazerbeam's skeleton.

The probe scanned the entire cave and then fixed on Gazerbeam's skeleton. Mr. Incredible held his breath and closed his eyes. The probe chirped and left.

Above the waterfall, the probe returned to Syndrome. "Life readings negative," it reported. "Mr. Incredible terminated."

Syndrome bowed his head in respect for his former idol and then chuckled wickedly.

Chapter 16

E led Helen downstairs to her secret lab. "This project has completely confiscated my life, darling . . . consumed me as only hero work can," E said with her usual enthusiasm. "My best work, I must admit. Simple. Elegant, yet bold. You will die. I did Robert's suit and it turned out so beautiful I just had to continue!"

"E," Helen said, "I have no idea what you're talking about. I just—"

"Yes, words are useless," E went on. "That is why I show you my work. That is why you are here!"

E turned to the wall. "Edna . . . Mode," she said into a microphone, and rapidly executed an elaborate series of security measures.

In a flash, a ceiling panel opened, revealing an enormous gun with its sights trained on Helen. E turned back to the microphone and added hastily, "*And* guest."

The gun retreated into the ceiling. The wall in front of them opened, revealing E's lab for designing and testing Super suits.

"Come, sit," E said, inviting Helen in for coffee. "Cream and sugar?" she asked.

Helen settled into a comfortable chair. She was about to ask E about Bob's Super suit when the lights in the lab suddenly dimmed. "I started with the baby," E said cheerfully.

"Started?" Helen asked.

"*Shhh,* darling, *shhh!*" E said as a small featureless baby mannequin in a tiny red suit emerged in a glass chamber, moving slowly from one side to the other.

"I cut it a little roomy for the free movement." E smiled.

The inside of the chamber erupted in flames. Helen jumped back.

"And," E added, "it can also withstand a temperature of over one thousand degrees!"

The flames were replaced by a barrage of machine-gun fire.

"Completely bulletproof and machine washable, darling. That's a new feature!"

Helen was shocked. "What in heaven's name do you think the baby will be doing?" she asked.

"Well, I'm sure I don't know, darling. Luck favors the prepared," E answered. "I didn't know the baby's powers, so I covered the basics."

"Jack-Jack doesn't have any powers," Helen said, staring at the little bulletproof suit.

"No? Well, he'll look fabulous anyway."

As the mannequin exited at one end, a mannequin of a young boy running at top speed appeared at the other end. The arms and legs accelerated until they blurred. "Your boy's suit," E said proudly. "I designed it to withstand enormous friction.

"Your daughter's suit was tricky," she continued as another mannequin entered. "I finally created a sturdy material that will disappear completely as she does."

All the red Super suits matched, and each had the letter *I* for *Incredible* emblazoned on the chest. Helen was stunned.

"Your suit can stretch as far as you can without injuring yourself and still retain its shape," E said, as if she was saving the best for last. A suit designed for Helen entered the chamber. Two giant robot arms appeared and clamped onto the arms of the new red Super suit on the mannequin. Two more clamped onto the pants, pulling and twisting them into every possible shape.

"Virtually indestructible!" E smiled. "Yet it breathes like Egyptian cotton. As an extra feature, each suit contains a homing device, giving you the precise global location of the wearer at the touch of a button."

The lights in E's design lab came up as the chamber went dark. "Well, darling? What do you think?" E asked.

"What do I think? Bob is retired! I'm retired! Our family is underground! You helped my husband resume secret hero work behind my back?"

"I assumed you knew, darling! Why would he keep secrets from you?" E asked.

"He wouldn't! He didn't—doesn't!" Helen stammered.

"Do you *know* where he is?" E replied, tilting her head.

Helen hesitated. "Of course."

E picked up her phone and handed it to Helen. "Do you *know* where he is?" she asked again.

Helen dialed Insuricare. "Hello, this is Helen Parr. Bob Parr is my husband. I was wondering if you could give me the number of the hotel he's staying at."

"Mr. Parr no longer works at Insuricare,"

the receptionist answered politely.

"What do you mean? He—he's on a business trip, a company retreat."

"My records say his employment was terminated almost two months ago."

Helen handed the phone back to E. Her face was expressionless.

"So," E said, shaking her head. "You don't know where he is. Would you like to find out?" she asked, holding up the homing device.

Helen hit the button on the homing device.

"I'm such an idiot!" Helen cried. "I let this happen, you know. The new sports car, the getting in shape!"

"Yes," E sighed. It was a familiar story. "He attempts to relive the past."

It was true. Helen knew Bob was happier when he was Mr. Incredible. "And now I am losing him!" she said. "What will I do? What will I do?"

"What are you talking about?" asked an impatient E. "*You are Elastigirl!* My God, pull yourself together! You will show him you remember that he is Mr. Incredible, and you will remind him who *you* are. You know where he is," she said, placing the homing device in Helen's hand. "Go. Confront the problem! *Fight! Win!*"

E walked Helen to the door. "And call me when you get back, darling. I enjoy our visits."

Chapter 17

At that moment on the island of Nomanisan, Mr. Incredible was calculating how he could get back into Syndrome's base unseen and disarm his control center.

Mr. Incredible caught hold of the next monopod streaking through the jungle and quickly got control of it from the guards. He zoomed to the front gates and entered the compound.

As soon as he was deeper inside the facility, he headed for the dining hall, the one place he knew held a secret passage to Syndrome's control room. Mr. Incredible stood in front of the lava falls, not knowing how to open it.

Finally, Mr. Incredible picked up a large stone statue at the end of the room and held it above his head. He was about to run into the lava, using the statue as a shield, when the falls suddenly parted. He struggled to replace the enormous statue to its original position and ducked behind it.

Mirage stepped out from the lava and walked across the room. The falls began to close.

Mr. Incredible rushed into the closing passage and jumped clear as the hot lava closed behind him.

He followed a series of floor lights that led to an elaborate chair in front of an enormous screen. He sat down and typed KRONOS into the controls.

Syndrome's plan to unleash his new and improved Omnidroid on the world flashed onto the screen, followed by the status of all the Supers that Syndrome had lured to the island. They'd all been done in by the evil mastermind. He had used them all as test subjects to perfect his Omnidroid. Mr. Incredible shook his head.

DYNAGUY: TERMINATED. GAZERBEAM: TERMINATED. The list went on and on.

Then Mr. Incredible saw FROZONE: LOCATION KNOWN. He suddenly thought of Helen. He searched for her name. ELASTIGIRL: LOCATION UNKNOWN. Mr. Incredible breathed a sigh of relief, but it was short-lived.

The homing device on his Super suit went off! An alarm sounded. Mr. Incredible tried to run out of the hall, but turrets came out of the walls and shot balls of sticky foam right at him. As the foam engulfed him, Mr. Incredible saw just one thing—Mirage's high-heeled shoes. He was caught!

Chapter 18

At the Parr house, Helen was preparing to take a trip.

"There's lots of leftovers you can reheat," she told Vi. "Make sure Dash does his homework and both of you get to bed on time. I should be back tonight, late. You can be in charge that long, can't you?" Helen asked.

"Yeah . . . but why am I in charge again?" Vi asked.

"Nothing. Just a little trouble with Daddy."

"You mean Dad's in trouble? Or Dad is the trouble?" Vi asked Helen.

"I mean either he's in trouble . . . or he's going to be," said Helen darkly as she walked into her bedroom.

Helen took a small duffel bag from the closet. She packed a few things and then held up her Super suit. She took a deep breath and stuffed the suit into her bag.

Dash did a double take as he passed her door. "Hey, what's *that*?" he asked, seeing the red suit.

"Where'd you get that, Mom?"

Helen stretched her arm to the door and closed it. Dash ran and immediately appeared outside the window. He looked at the matching red suits laid out on the bed.

"Hey, are those for us? We all get cool outfits?" he asked, intrigued.

Helen took her hand off the door and stretched it to shut the blinds. Dash zoomed back through the door, nabbed his Super suit, and was gone.

"Wait a—Dash! You come back *this moment*!" Helen yelled as the phone rang.

It was her friend Snug, the owner and pilot of some of the fastest jet planes ever to fly. Helen knew Snug from the old days.

"Hey, Snug! Thanks for getting back. Listen, I know this is short notice, but I'm calling in a solid you owe me," Helen said into the phone.

"Whaddya need?" Snug asked.

"A jet," Helen said calmly. "What can you get that's fast?"

"Let me think," said Snug.

Violet walked into her mom's bedroom.

"What are these?" she asked, staring at the red suits on the bed.

Suddenly, Dash appeared.

"Look!" he said proudly, wearing his Super suit and smiling at himself in the mirror. "I'm 'The Dash'!"

"Just a moment," Helen said to Snug, and placed her hand over the mouthpiece. "Take that off, before somebody sees you," she ordered.

"But you're packing one just like it," Vi said, pointing to the red suit in Helen's bag. "Are you hiding something?"

"Please, honey, I'm on the phone," Helen pleaded.

Dash picked up Vi's suit and handed it to her. "This is yours!" he told her. "It's specially made."

"What's going on?" Violet asked, dropping her shoulders and turning to her mom. Helen pushed them both into the hall and closed the door.

Vi was still holding her Super suit. "What makes you think it's special?" she asked Dash as they stood in the hall.

"I dunno. Why'd Mom try to hide it?" Dash replied matter-of-factly before running off.

Vi looked down at her suit and wondered. Then, making her hand invisible, she touched a finger to it. The suit disappeared in her hand.

"Whoa," said Vi.

It had been a long time since Helen had flown a jet—but it all came back to her quickly. "Island approach, India Golf Niner Niner checking in, VFR on top. Over," she said into her headset. She had tracked Bob through the homing device to the small volcanic island below, but the landing tower didn't answer.

Helen tried again. "Island tower. This is India, Golf, Niner, Niner requesting vectors!" Still no one responded.

Helen began to feel a little nervous. "Easy," she told herself. "You're overreacting. Everything's fine." Five seconds later, she put the jet on autopilot and grabbed her Super suit.

As Helen flew toward the island of Nomanisan, Mr. Incredible awoke and found himself in Syndrome's prison chamber, his arms and legs bound by metal restraints that held him suspended by Syndrome's immobi-ray technology. Syndrome stood triumphant over his captured hero.

"You, sir, truly are Mr. Incredible," Syndrome said enthusiastically. "You know, I was right to idolize you. I always knew you were tough. But tricking the probe by hiding under the bones of another Super? Ohhhh, man! I'm still geeking out about it!"

Syndrome's face suddenly soured. "Then you had to go and just—ruin the ride." He shook his head. "I mean, Mr. Incredible calling for help? 'Help me!' Lame, lame, lame, lame, *lame*! Who did you contact?"

"Contact? What are you talking about?" asked Mr. Incredible.

With a nod from Syndrome, a jolt of electricity went into Mr. Incredible's chest. He winced in pain.

"I'm referring to last night at 2307 hours, while you were snooping around, you sent out a homing signal," Syndrome said impatiently, and jolted Mr. Incredible again.

"I didn't—" said Mr. Incredible painfully.

"And now a government plane is requesting permission to land here! *Who did you contact?*" Syndrome demanded in a rage.

"I didn't send for . . . a plane." Mr. Incredible grimaced.

"Play the transmission," said Syndrome to Mirage.

"Island approach, India Golf Niner Niner checking in, VFR on top."

Mr. Incredible's head snapped up. "Helen!" he said.

"So you do know these people," Syndrome said, smiling maliciously. "Well then, I'll send them a little greeting." He pressed LAUNCH on the console and began to laugh.

"No!" shouted Mr. Incredible, but he was helpless.

Chapter 19

Helen changed into her Super suit and tossed her duffel bag into a passenger seat.

"Ow!"

"Violet!" Helen said angrily as her daughter rematerialized.

"It's not my fault!" Violet explained as fast as she could. "Dash ran away and I knew I'd get blamed for it and—"

"That's not true!" Dash loudly interrupted, popping up from behind a seat. Helen threw her arms in the air. They were both in the plane. "*You* said, 'Something's up with Mom,'" Dash continued hotly, "and, 'We hafta find out what,' and it was *your idea, your idea, one hundred percent all yours all the time idea!*"

"I thought he'd try to sneak on the plane so I came here and you closed the doors before I could find him and then you took off," Violet argued. "It's *not my fault*!"

Helen's expression suddenly changed. "Wait a minute, you left Jack-Jack alone?" she asked them.

“Yes, Mom! I’m completely stupid,” Violet said sarcastically. “Of course we got a sitter! Do you think I’m totally irresponsible? Thanks a lot!”

“Well, who’d you get?” asked Helen anxiously as she dialed home.

“You don’t have to worry about one single thing, Mrs. Parr. I’ve got this babysitting thing wired,” Jack-Jack’s new thirteen-year-old babysitter said.

“Kari?” said Helen uncertainly.

“I also brought Mozart to play while he sleeps because leading experts say Mozart makes babies smarter,” Kari continued.

“Kari—” Helen interrupted.

“—and the beauty part is the babies don’t even have to listen ’cause they’re asleep!”

“Kari, I really don’t feel comfortable with this. I’ll pay you for your trouble, but I’d really rather call a service.”

“There’s really no need, Mrs. Parr. I can handle anything this baby can dish out. Can’t I, little boobily boy?” Kari cooed at Jack-Jack.

A warning signal sounded from the cockpit. Helen’s eyes widened. She ran to the cockpit. The white trail of a missile—coming straight for them—was visible above the clouds.

Helen grabbed the headset as the rocket roared toward them. "Friendlies at two-zero miles south-southwest of your position, disengage. Over!" Helen yelled into the headset. "Disengage!"

Dash and Vi exchanged frantic glances. The red light above their heads flashed FASTEN SEAT BELTS. Panicked, they tried to buckle in, but it was too late. The jet took a dive, slamming them to the ceiling. The missile smoked by as Helen tried to call for help.

The jet was in a dive, the ocean coming straight at them. Helen yanked back on the controls. The nose came up enough for the plane to skim the waves before it finally turned upward.

Helen saw two more missiles appear on her screen. She whirled around to Violet.

"Vi! You have to put a force field around the plane!" Helen shouted.

"But you said we weren't supposed to use our powers—" Violet protested.

"I know what I said," Helen told her. "Listen to what I'm saying now!"

In the prison cell, Mr. Incredible had heard the entire radio transmission.

"I've never done one that big before!" he heard Violet say.

Then he heard Helen shout, *"Violet! Do it now!"*

"Call off the missiles! I'll do anything!" Mr. Incredible yelled.

"Too late," Syndrome told him coldly. "Fifteen years too late."

Inside the jet, Helen turned back to the radar screen. The missiles were closing in fast. There was no time left.

Helen threw off the headset and leaped out of her seat. She stretched herself around her two children.

Mr. Incredible saw the missile register a hit on the radar screen. He closed his eyes in grief and horror.

Chapter 20

Syndrome smiled as Mirage confirmed that the target was destroyed. Mr. Incredible was crushed. Helen and the kids were gone. "Ah, you'll get over it," Syndrome said to him. "I seem to recall you prefer to 'work alone.'"

In a sudden burst of rage, Mr. Incredible lunged at Syndrome. Mirage pushed Syndrome away, but Mr. Incredible managed to grab her instead.

"Release me. Now!" Mr. Incredible growled as a guard turned up the control panel, suspending Mirage and Mr. Incredible in the chamber.

"Or what?" said Syndrome.

"I'll crush her," Mr. Incredible said, squeezing Mirage tightly.

"Sounds a little dark for you." Syndrome laughed. "Go ahead."

"No!" Mirage cried.

"It'll be easy," Mr. Incredible said. "Like breaking a toothpick."

"Show me," Syndrome said smugly.

Mr. Incredible hesitated, gritted his teeth, then

let Mirage go. Syndrome laughed as Mirage fell to the floor.

"I knew you couldn't do it. Even when you have nothing to lose, you're weak. I've outgrown you," he said in disgust, and walked out.

Meanwhile, far out over the ocean, the smoke from the missile's explosion began to disperse. Then an orange-red ball emerged from the blast and began to unfurl. It was Helen back in action as Elastigirl. Dash and Vi were plummeting fast beneath her. Elastigirl quickly stretched herself into a human parachute as she grabbed both her children in midair, breaking their fall as they splashed into the water below.

Dash and Vi broke the water's surface, sputtering and splashing.

"Mom!"

"Everybody calm down," Helen told them as they struggled to stay afloat. "We're not going to panic!"

But on the ocean, Dash and Vi couldn't help it. Panic began to overtake them.

"We're dead! We're dead!" Dash cried, treading water. "We survived, but we're dead!"

"Stop it!" shouted Helen. "We are not going to die! Now, both of you will get a grip or so help me I'll ground you for a month! Understand?"

Dash and Vi looked at their mom; then both nodded at the same time.

"Those were short-range missiles," Helen told them as they bobbed in the water. "Land based. That way is our best bet." She pointed at the missile trails.

"You want to go toward the people that tried to kill us?" asked Dash.

"If it means land . . . yes."

"Do you expect us to swim there?" asked Violet.

"I expect you to trust me," Helen told them.

Dash and Vi watched, amazed, as their mother stretched her body into the shape of a boat. They both climbed on board. Helen had Dash put his legs over the side and kick them at Super speed. The Parr family boat was moving toward the island of Nomanisan.

It was sunset when they reached the beach. "What a trooper," Helen said as she reached over to hug Dash. He was exhausted. "I'm so proud of you."

"Thanks, Mom." Dash smiled wearily.

Cold and wet, Helen and the kids found a cave in the volcanic rock and built a fire to warm themselves as the sun went down.

"I think your father is in trouble," Helen told Dash and Vi as they huddled around the fire. "I'm going to look for him. That means you're in charge until I get back, Violet."

"What?" asked Dash.

"You heard her," Vi said.

Helen reached into the battered duffel bag.

"Put these on," she said, handing them their black masks. "Your identity is your most valuable possession. Protect it. If anything goes wrong, use your powers."

"But you said never to use—" began Violet.

Helen sighed. "Remember the bad guys on those shows you used to watch on Saturday mornings? Well, these guys are not like those guys. They will kill you. Do *not* give them that chance. Vi, I'm counting on you."

Helen turned to Dash. "Be strong," she told him. "If anything goes wrong, I want you to run as fast as you can."

"As fast as I can?" Dash asked, making sure.

"As fast as you can," Helen told him. "Stay hidden. Keep each other safe. I'll be back by morning."

Helen gave them both a long hug and turned to leave. Vi ran after her.

"Mom . . . what happened on the plane . . . ," Vi said with tears in her eyes. She knew her force field could have helped if she had just been confident enough to try. "I—couldn't—I'm—I didn't—I'm so sorry."

Helen placed a finger over Vi's lips and tilted her head.

"Shhh," she told her. "It wasn't fair for me to suddenly ask so much of you. But things are different now. And doubt is a luxury we can't afford anymore, sweetie."

Then Helen smiled. "You have more power than you realize. And don't worry. If the time comes, you'll know what to do. It's in your blood."

At the same time that Dash and Vi were watching Helen disappear into the dark jungle, Mirage was outside Mr. Incredible's cell door, talking to Syndrome.

"He's not weak, you know," Mirage said.

"What?" snapped Syndrome.

Mirage rubbed the back of her neck. "Valuing life is not weakness," she said softly.

“Hey, if you’re talking about what happened—” Syndrome began as he waved a hand toward Mr. Incredible’s cell.

Mirage snapped her head up. “And disregarding it is not strength,” she said accusingly.

“I called his bluff.” Syndrome shrugged. “I knew he wouldn’t—”

But Mirage was already walking away. “Next time you gamble,” she said coldly, “bet your own life.”

Elastigirl fluidly moved through the dense jungle, occasionally pulling herself from tree to tree with her outstretched arms. Making her way into a clearing, she saw the glint of a gray steel monorail overhead. Then she heard the hum of a monopod approaching in the distance.

Elastigirl threw her arms up high as the lights of the monopod streaked above her. Her hands gripped the vehicle, and it yanked her feet from the jungle floor. She dangled from the monopod until she could swing herself to its top.

The pod sliced through the jungle canopy with Elastigirl determined to hang on. As she squinted into the wind, she could see that the monopod was speeding toward the base of a towering volcano. The pod plunged into a dark tunnel and emerged inside a room with a massive launchpad. "A rocket?" Elastigirl wondered. She decided it was time to drop in and investigate.

Finding a corridor off the launchpad, Elastigirl stretched her neck and looked around a corner.

A guard was sliding a key card through a reader, and *whoosh,* the door in front of him opened. She needed that key card. It would let her access different parts of Syndrome's lair to look for her husband.

But as Elastigirl stretched toward the guard holding the key card, the doors behind her snapped shut, trapping her leg. Soon more guards approached, opening more doors, and Elastigirl found herself caught in two separate doorways—her torso in one, and her leg still in the other. Using her Super elasticity, she managed to kick and punch all the guards till they were unconscious.

She grabbed a key card, freed herself, and set off down the corridor once again. It was time to find her husband.

Chapter 22

Inside the cave, Dash and Vi sat close to the fire. Dash stared into space as Vi practiced generating force fields over the fire. Each try was like a little bubble.

"Well, not that this isn't fun," Dash finally said, "but I'm gonna go look around."

Vi stood up. "What do you think is going on here? You think we're on vacation or something? Mom and Dad's lives could be in jeopardy. Mom said to stay hidden."

Dash rolled his eyes. "I'm not gonna leave the cave," he said, annoyed.

He grumbled as he took a flaming stick and moved into the darkness. Vi could see the flame getting smaller as Dash moved farther and farther away. "Cool . . . ," she heard him say in the far distance. Then suddenly . . . she heard Dash scream.

"Vi! Vi, Vi, Vi, Vi, Vi!" Dash yelled, running back toward her at warp speed.

"What?" said Violet as Dash pointed to an orange glow at one end of the cave. It was growing brighter and brighter, getting closer and closer. Vi could feel the heat of it on her face. "What did you *do*?" she screamed as they both raced out of the cave.

Dash and Vi outran the fireball in time to see a rocket roar into the sky. Looking up, they realized they hadn't been hiding in a cave at all. It was the exhaust tunnel for the rocket launch.

That night, they had no choice but to sleep on the jungle floor.

Dash awoke to the exotic sounds of the jungle. He stretched his legs, still stiff from the day before. Suddenly, he heard the words "Identification, please." He rubbed his eyes and looked up. The words had come from a brilliantly colored robotic bird perched in a nearby tree. Dash watched it, mesmerized.

He was thrilled. "Hey, Violet!" He laughed, nudging his sister. "Look! It talks!"

"Huh? What?" Vi answered, still sleepy.

Vi tilted her head and smiled. They stared at the bird, enchanted, waiting for it to speak again.

"Voice key incorrect," the bird said.

"Voice key?" Vi repeated, and frowned.

The bird's head mechanically swiveled toward Dash and Vi. Its eyes lit up red as its beak dropped open and it let out a shrill electronic alarm.

"What do we do?" asked Dash as Vi began to back away.

"Run!" yelled Violet.

"Where are we going?" said Dash, hesitating.

"Away from here!" she called back.

Chapter 23

The silhouette of a slender woman appeared in Mr. Incredible's cell. She walked to the control panel and switched off the immobi-ray. "There isn't much time," she told Mr. Incredible, who dropped to his knees. It was Mirage.

"No, there isn't," Mr. Incredible said, grabbing Mirage's throat. "There's no time at all."

"Please . . . ," Mirage gasped.

In a fury, Mr. Incredible lashed out. "Why are you here? How can you possibly bring me lower? What more can you take away from me?"

"F-f-amily . . . survived the crash . . . ," Mirage gasped. "They're here—on the island."

"They're alive?" Mr. Incredible said, astounded. Overjoyed, he stood up and threw his arms around Mirage.

Mr. Incredible opened his eyes and saw another woman standing in the doorway. "Helen!" he cried.

Mirage stepped back. She was about to say hello when Elastigirl's fist flew across the room. Mirage fell hard.

"She was helping me to escape," Bob said, trying to explain.

"No, that's what I was doing!" Helen replied.

Bob took Helen in his arms.

"Let go of me, you unfaithful creep," Helen protested.

"How could I betray the perfect woman?" he said. "Where are the kids?"

Mirage sat up and rubbed her jaw. "They might have triggered the alert," she told them. "Security's been sent into the jungle. You'd better get going."

Bob and Helen headed for the door. "Now our kids are in danger," Helen said, still upset by the whole situation.

"If you suspected danger, why'd you bring them?" Bob asked as he began to run.

"I didn't bring them," Helen said, running right next to him. "They stowed away, and I don't think you're striking the proper tone here."

Chapter 24

At that moment, Dash and Vi were running blindly through the jungle. Almost out of breath, they stopped dead in their tracks. Three high-speed velocipods were in their path. Vi spoke calmly in a low voice as she looked into the faces of the armed guards. "Dash. Remember what Mom said."

"What?" Dash asked, terrified, remembering the part about these guys not being like the bad guys you watched on TV. Then Vi disappeared.

"Dash! *Run!*" Vi shouted.

Right! Dash thought as he bolted into the jungle.

"They're *Supers*!" one of the guards yelled. *"Get the boy!"*

Dash ran at lightning speed, the velocipods hot on his trail. The vines and undergrowth were so dense that Dash was forced to stick to a narrow jungle trail. Suddenly, he rocketed through a thick, dark cloud. It was a swarm of black jungle flies. *"Aggcchh!"* Dash choked as the flies hit his face like bugs smashing into a windshield. He shook his head and tumbled into the undergrowth. He sat up and rubbed his bug-spattered teeth with the back of his sleeve.

"Achppt! *Ptthwaaagh! Pthtp!*" sputtered Dash, spitting bits of fly wings and legs from his mouth.

The velocipods suddenly burst through the undergrowth, and Dash began tearing through the jungle again. He saw a hanging vine ahead and reached for it as he zoomed by. Dash swung around in a wide arc, surprising the last velocipod and causing it to veer off into the undergrowth. Immediately, another velocipod was hot on his trail. Dash grabbed another vine and was propelled forward. But the vine snapped and he rose into the air, suddenly realizing that he was no longer over land. He was falling fast off the edge of a cliff! Dash screamed.

With a thud, he landed on the hood of a velocipod. He couldn't believe his luck. He was okay! A guard turned and took a swing at him. But Dash used his Super speed to duck every punch. He was beginning to get comfortable with his Super powers. He even managed to get in a few high-speed punches himself.

Dash was feeling pretty proud until he realized

that the velocipod was headed straight for a cliff wall. The guard suddenly socked Dash in the jaw, knocking him off the vehicle. Dash watched the velocipod slam into the cliff wall, vaporizing into a ball of fire.

Dash fell through the trees below the cliff. He hit branch after branch as he fell flailing through an enormous tree. He tried to grab anything to stop his fall and finally got his hands around a vine. Dash hung from the vine. Then he looked down. He was about three feet off the jungle floor. How had he ever survived that? He dropped to the ground and let out a loud whoop in victory.

Two nearby guards on velocipods turned and headed toward the sound. The velocipods picked up Dash's trail as he ran toward a lagoon. Dash charged straight ahead and took a deep breath. He was ready to get wet, but when he looked down, he was surprised. He was running fast enough to skim along the water's surface.

Dash blasted across the lagoon, weaving like a speedboat around the volcanic rocks jutting out of the water. One velocipod followed as he darted into a cave. Dash realized he was in a tunnel when he saw the second velocipod coming at him from the other side. He frantically looked for a way out. He was trapped. Dash stopped running and dropped beneath the water's surface. He was relieved when he heard the *boom!* of the two velocipods colliding overhead.

A guard scanned the area with his rifle, looking for any sign of Violet. Invisible, Violet quickly clubbed the guard, knocking away his rifle and giving herself just enough time to run into the jungle.

"Show yourself!" he commanded.

He picked up his gun and fired, unleashing a barrage of bullets at a series of footprints that streaked toward the river. The guard heard a splash and fired at a rippling mass under the water's surface.

He reached down, grabbed a handful of dirt, and threw it into the river. Violet's outline showed clearly in the murky water. The guard smiled, raised his rifle, and took aim.

But Vi didn't stay still—she splashed out of the river and made a run for the jungle. The guard swung his gun toward her. At that moment, Dash darted from the jungle, running full throttle toward the guard's legs.

"Don't touch my sister!" Dash shouted as he knocked the guard down. The guard managed to get a punch in as the two tumbled. Stunned for a moment, Dash looked up to see the rifle pointed at his chest. The guard smiled and the trigger clicked. Violet leaped between them, throwing a force field around her and Dash, protecting them. Dash was amazed. Violet floated in midair, suspended in her own force field.

"How are you doing that?" Dash asked as the bullets from the guard ricocheted off the force field.

"I don't know!" Vi answered.

"Whatever you do—*don't stop!*" Dash said enthusiastically.

Dash began to run within the force field like a gerbil in a wheel, causing them to roll into the jungle, rumbling past the guards and down a hillside.

Chapter 25

Mr. Incredible and Elastigirl raced through the jungle side by side. "I should have told you I was fired, I admit it," Mr. Incredible said, trying to apologize, "but I didn't want you to worry."

"You didn't want me to worry?" Elastigirl exclaimed. "And now we're running for our lives through some godforsaken jungle!"

But Mr. Incredible just shook his head and smiled. "You keep trying to pick a fight, but I'm still just happy you're alive."

Mr. Incredible and Elastigirl heard an explosion echo through the jungle, followed by a deep rumble that grew louder and louder. Suddenly, the rolling force field with Dash and Vi, having just barely escaped two chasing velocipods, burst out of the jungle in front of them.

"Mom! Dad!" Dash and Vi yelled.

The force field flattened Mr. Incredible and Elastigirl like cookie dough against a rolling pin. "Kids!"

Violet disintegrated the force field, and the

family fell to the ground, hugging wildly.

Suddenly, a velocipod blasted out of the jungle. The Incredibles jumped to their feet and faced the fight together.

Elastigirl threw a stretched scissor kick that caught a guard in the chest, knocking him out of his velocipod. In perfect harmony, Mr. Incredible threw a chop at a second passing velocipod and sent it plowing into the jungle floor. Elastigirl coiled her arm around the pod's pilot and whiplashed him into another guard, knocking them both out cold. Mr. Incredible grabbed the crashed velocipod and threw it into another that had just emerged from the trees. Mr. Incredible and Elastigirl looked around at the crashed velocipods that now littered the jungle floor.

"I love you," they were saying to each other with admiration when the jungle suddenly filled with guards. The whole family reacted in a blur of Super powers. The guards were no match for the Incredibles.

"Whoa, whoa, *whoa!*" Syndrome said, stepping out of the jungle. *"Time out!"* he shouted, firing his immobi-ray and suspending the Incredibles motionless in midair.

Syndrome crossed his arms and assessed the scene. "What have we here?" he asked, amused. "Matching uniforms?"

He narrowed his eyes and looked at Elastigirl.

"Oh, no!" He laughed out loud. "Elastigirl? You married Elastigirl? And got *biz-zay*!" he said to Mr. Incredible. "It's a whole family of Supers! Looks like I've hit the jackpot! Oh, this is just *too good*!" he exclaimed, relishing the moment.

Chapter 26

Inside Syndrome's prison chamber, Mr. Incredible, Elastigirl, Dash, and Vi were held captive in immobi-rays, side by side. On a giant screen in front of them, a newscast showed a crowd gathered around a large smoldering craft at the base of a building. The Omnidroid had landed in the city. The Incredibles had no choice but to watch.

"Huh?" Syndrome said, seeing their reaction to the destruction of Metroville. "Oh, come on, you gotta admit this is cool! Just like a movie! The robot will emerge dramatically, do some damage, throngs of screaming people, and just when all hope is lost, Syndrome will save the day. I'll be a bigger hero than you ever were!"

"You killed off real heroes so that you could pretend to be one?" Mr. Incredible asked him.

"Oh, I'm real enough to defeat you!" Syndrome said cynically. "And I did it without your precious gifts. Your oh-so-special powers."

Syndrome continued excitedly, "I'll give them heroics. I'll give them the most spectacular heroics the world has ever seen." Syndrome cackled darkly. "And when I'm old, I'll sell my inventions so that everyone can be Super. And when everyone's Super, no one will be." He exited in triumph as Bob hung his head. "I'm sorry," he said to his family. Helen and the kids looked up.

"This is my fault," Bob said. "I've been a lousy father. Blind . . . to what I have."

As Bob spoke, he didn't notice Vi moving. She was suspended in her own force field and no longer in the immobi-rays. She began to roll toward the control panel. "So obsessed with being undervalued that I undervalued all of you," Bob continued, lost in his own confession.

"Dad," Dash said.

"Shhh! Don't interrupt," Helen said.

"So caught up in the past that I . . . I . . . You are my greatest adventure. And I almost missed it," Bob said as Vi dissipated the force field around her. "I swear I'm gonna get us out of this safely."

Vi suddenly spoke as she placed her hand on the control panel. "Well, I think Dad has made some excellent progress today . . . but I think it's time we wind down now." Bob looked at his daughter, stunned.

Vi threw a switch and the beam flickered off, dropping Bob, Helen, and Dash to the floor. Vi had saved the family!

The Incredibles raced through an empty corridor. "We need to get back to the mainland," Bob said.

"I saw an aircraft hangar on my way in," Helen said. "Straight ahead, I think."

They came to the hangar door and Bob quickly pried it open, expecting swarms of guards on the other side. But no one was to be found.

"Where are all the guards?" he asked.

Then he heard cheers from inside a mobile command vehicle parked in the hangar bay. The guards were inside, watching the Omnidroid attack the city on the news and celebrating.

Bob entered the vehicle alone. The door closed behind him. When he came out, all of the guards had been knocked out. He whistled to his family, who were hiding behind the vehicle.

"This is the right hangar," Helen said, "but I don't see any jets."

"A jet's not fast enough," Bob said, knowing Syndrome had a good head start.

"How about a rocket?" Dash suggested, pointing to a rocket in the launching bay.

"I can't fly a rocket," Helen said.

"You don't have to," Vi told her. "Use the coordinates from the last launch."

Bob and Helen looked at each other, beaming over their clever daughter.

"I'll bet Syndrome's changed the password by now," Bob said suddenly. "How do I get into the computer?"

A woman's voice came over the loudspeaker. "Say please." The Incredibles looked up. It was Mirage. She stood at the monitoring station, smiling.

Chapter 27

In Metroville, Lucius Best was dressing for a dinner engagement. He was putting on cologne when he thought he heard a series of explosions. Suddenly, Lucius saw a huge six-legged Omnidroid outside his window. He began opening his dresser drawers.

"Honey?" he called to his wife in the other room.

"What?" Honey answered.

"Where's my Super suit?"

"What?" Honey asked.

"Where is my Super suit?" Lucius demanded.

"I put it away!" she shouted to him.

"Where?" he said, going through the drawers as the Omnidroid filled the window.

"Why do you need to know?"

"The public is in danger!" Lucius shouted.

"My evening's in danger!" Honey said firmly.

"You tell me where my suit is, woman! We're talking about the greater good!"

"Greater good?" she shouted back. "I am

your wife! I am the greatest good you are ever going to get!"

Out on the streets of Metroville, the city's new Super, Syndrome, had the situation well in hand.

"Stand back!" Syndrome told the crowd. "Someone needs to teach this hunk of metal a few manners!"

Syndrome faked a punch while he secretly used the remote on his wrist to send a signal to the arm of the Omnidroid, which fell out of its socket, crashing into the street. The crowd went wild. Syndrome reveled in their cheers of appreciation. The Omnidroid, however, was still a learning robot.

CONTROL STOLEN BY EXTERNAL SIGNAL, the robot began to process. It crunched the numbers and slowly turned toward Syndrome.

SIGNAL SOURCE: REMOTE CONTROL, it concluded. The robot shot a laser at the remote control, knocking it from Syndrome's wrist. Syndrome's eyes grew wide. Then the robot shot a laser at Syndrome's rocket boots. The hot laser blasted the boots, causing Syndrome to lose control and sending him wildly careening into a building, where he was knocked unconscious. The

Omnidroid went back to thrashing the city without interference.

Chapter 28

High above Metroville, another rocket shot across the sky. A landing craft broke away from the rocket, but it wasn't another Omnidroid. The landing craft was carrying the mobile command vehicle from the island. It looked a lot like a family van, but this was no vacation. Bob was at the wheel.

"Are we there yet?" Dash asked from the backseat.

"We get there when we get there!" Bob said impatiently.

Bob rolled down the window and leaned his head out. Helen was stretched to the max on top of the mobile command vehicle. She was using her elastic body to keep it attached to the landing craft. "How you doing, honey?"

"Do I have to answer?" a very stretched-out Helen replied.

"Kids!" Bob shouted. "Strap yourselves down like I told you!" he said. "This is going to be rough."

He poked his head out the window and shouted

to Helen, "Here we go, honey!"

Helen released her hold on the landing craft as the van was disengaged. It now streaked through the sky and was headed for the freeway. The van hit the pavement in a shower of sparks, doing two hundred miles an hour. Bob struggled to maintain control as he hit the brakes. Tires smoking, he steered the van into freeway traffic.

"The robot is in the financial district," he said, his heart racing. "Which exit do I take?"

"Traction Avenue," Helen said from the passenger seat.

Bob cut across three lanes of traffic like a bullet, heading for the Seventh Avenue exit. "That'll take me downtown! I take Seventh, don't I?"

"Don't take Seventh!" Helen yelled.

"Great!" Bob said, furious. "We missed it!"

"You asked me how to get there and I told you: exit at Traction!"

"That'll take me downtown!" Bob insisted.

"It's coming up! Get in the right lane! *Signal!*" Helen screamed.

Bob changed into the left lane again. "We don't exit at Traction!"

"You're gonna miss it!" Helen warned.

At the last possible second, Bob swerved across the freeway.

"*Eeewhyaaaahhhh!*" Bob yelled as the van hit the guardrail, barely making the exit.

Chapter 29

Bob struggled to keep control of the van as it careened down the street. He hit the brakes, the tires blew, and the vehicle overturned and tumbled down the street, coming to rest perfectly in a parking spot. "Is everybody all right?"

"Super-duper, Dad," Vi said.

"Let's do that again!" Dash laughed.

The family watched the Omnidroid disappear between some buildings. "Wait here and stay hidden," Bob told them. "I'm going in."

"While what?" Helen asked, following him out of the vehicle. "I watch helplessly from the sidelines? I don't think so."

"I'm asking you to wait with the kids."

"And I'm telling you, not a chance," Helen insisted. "You're my husband. I'm with you. For better or worse."

"I have to do this alone," Bob said sternly.

"What is this to you? Playtime?" Helen asked.

"No," Bob said.

"So you can be Mr. Incredible again?"

"No!" Bob snapped.

"Then what?" Helen asked, confused. "What is it?"

"I'm . . . I'm not . . . not strong enough!" Bob said finally.

"Strong enough?" Helen asked. "And this will make you stronger? *That's* what this is? Some sort of workout?"

"I can't lose you again!" Bob shouted at Helen. "I can't," he whispered. "Not again . . . I'm not strong enough."

Helen was stunned. She leaned over and kissed him. "If we work together," she said, "you won't have to be."

"I don't know what'll happen," Bob said.

"Hey, we're Supers." Helen smiled. "What could happen?"

Suddenly, the raging Omnidroid was looming over Dash and Violet.

"Vi! Dash! No!" Helen shouted.

But it was too late. The Omnidroid pounced on the kids with its full weight. Helen froze. She could barely see Dash and Vi beneath the enormous robot. But something was keeping the Omnidroid from crushing the kids completely. A force field! Vi was keeping her brother and herself safe by projecting a protective force field around them.

The robot pressed hard on Vi's force field. So hard that she knocked her head on its metal bottom and the force field vanished.

"Violet!" Dash yelled.

Mr. Incredible went into action. He quickly wedged himself under the robot, holding it off the kids.

"Go! Go!" Mr. Incredible shouted, barely raising the Omnidroid.

Dash and Vi took off toward Elastigirl, who told them to stay put as she headed out to help her husband. Just then, the robot picked up Mr. Incredible and threw him into a glass building. Mr. Incredible got up and lunged toward the robot, landing a powerful punch.

In the same instant, the sun flashed off the surface of a blue bolt made of ice.

"Frozone!" Mr. Incredible yelled, happy to see his Super buddy gliding on a path of ice toward the Omnidroid. Help was on the way!

Mr. Incredible turned back toward his foe and landed a powerful punch on the robot, but it backhanded him into the side of a building.

Mr. Incredible shook off the momentary pain and noticed Syndrome's remote lying on the ground. He couldn't believe his good luck. The remote controlled everything on the Omnidroid—if only he could figure out how to work it. He grabbed the gadget just as the Omnidroid got its metal claw around him and lifted him high into the air.

Mr. Incredible pressed a button on the remote. The Omnidroid's arm instantly dropped into the street and released Mr. Incredible. The robot was still fighting for the remote when Mr. Incredible got an idea.

"Dash, go long!" he shouted to his son. Dash headed down the street in a blur as Mr. Incredible threw the remote like a football. The Super-speedy kid reached the gadget just in time.

But now the Omnidroid went after Dash. The robot used its laser to trap Dash in a ring of burning cars.

"Take out its guns!" Mr. Incredible yelled to Elastigirl.

Elastigirl flung a manhole cover at the robot, destroying its laser beam, as Frozone swooped in to rescue Dash. The Omnidroid thundered down the street after them. The learning robot knew it needed to get the remote back.

Then it was Frozone's turn to help out. He cut across the river, freezing a path and taking Dash along. The Omnidroid vaulted into the air and nearly landed on them. Ice chunks sent Frozone and Dash tumbling while the remote spun out of Dash's hand. Mr. Incredible charged forward to grab it, but the robot fired its claw at him, trapping him down the street in its metal pincers.

Then the remote seemingly moved by itself.

"Mom! I've got it!" Vi shouted, holding it in her invisible hand. "I've got the remote!"

"A remote?" Frozone asked. "A remote that controls what? The robot?"

"It's getting closer," Dash warned as the Omnidroid bore down upon them.

"It's not working," said Violet, desperately pushing buttons on the remote. Her mother and Dash soon joined in, all trying various combinations of buttons, hoping to destroy the Omnidroid.

"That's not doing anything. Try the one next to it. The red one!" Frozone argued.

The robot kept coming after them, but the remote did open the claw that had Mr. Incredible pinned down the street. He realized that the only thing that could penetrate and destroy the robot was itself. Suddenly, a rocket at the end of the claw was activated. That gave Mr. Incredible an idea. He struggled to control the claw and looked down the street toward his family and Frozone. The Omnidroid was bearing down on them.

Mr. Incredible pointed the claw and yelled to his family, "Duck!" The rocket fired, and the claw flew right through the center of the Omnidroid. It fell in the river in a mass of sparks and explosions as the Supers and the citizens of Metroville watched its every circuit blow.

The crowds cheered. The Supers were back!

Chapter 30

The Incredibles were heroes again. They were driven home first class in the company of Rick Dicker, the government's Super relocation handler. "The people of this country owe you all a debt of gratitude," Rick said. "We'll make good on it."

"Does this mean we can come out of hiding?" Bob asked hopefully.

"Let the politicians figure that one out," Rick said. "But I've been asked to assure you we'll take care of everything else. You did good, Bob."

Meanwhile, Helen was on the cell phone, checking the messages. The first was from Kari, the babysitter.

"Hello, Mrs. Parr. Everything's fine, but there's something unusual about Jack-Jack. Call me, okay?"

Bob sat back, relaxed for the first time in ages. He looked at his daughter.

"You're wearing your hair back," he said to her, smiling.

"Huh? Oh . . . yeah," Vi said, touching her hair. "I just . . . yeah."

"It looks good," he said.

"Thanks, Dad," Violet said, blushing.

"That was so cool when you threw that car," Dash said, remembering the battle against Syndrome's guards in the jungle.

"Not as cool as you running on water," Bob told Dash.

"And, Mom," Dash went on, "that was sweet when you snagged that bad guy with your arm and kinda, like, whiplashed him into the other guy."

Helen smiled. "I'm trying to listen to messages, honey."

Dash fell back in his seat, exclaiming, "That was the best vacation ever! I love our family!"

Helen covered her ear, trying to hear the next message. "It's me!" Kari said. "Jack-Jack's fine but I'm really getting weirded out! *When are you coming back? Call me, okay?*"

"Bob, listen to this," Helen said, suddenly concerned. Bob leaned in to hear the message: "Hi, this is Kari. Sorry for freaking out. But your baby has special needs. Anyway, thanks for sending a replacement sitter."

Bob and Helen exchanged worried looks.

Chapter 31

Bob and Helen opened their front door and saw the replacement sitter.

"*Shhh.* The baby's sleeping," Syndrome said, holding Jack-Jack in his arms.

"You took away my future," he said calmly. "I'm simply returning the favor. Don't worry. I'll be a good mentor: supportive, encouraging. Everything you weren't."

Jack-Jack woke up and began to cry. "And in time, who knows?" Syndrome smiled. "He might make a good sidekick."

Syndrome blasted a hole in the roof. A jet was hovering high above the house. Syndrome activated his rocket boots and zoomed upward with Jack-Jack crying in his arms.

As he neared the jet, a hatch opened. He was about to duck in when Jack-Jack's cries became louder and louder and *louder.* Syndrome froze as Jack-Jack suddenly transformed from fire to a hideous screaming mini-monster.

Horrified, Syndrome tried to drop the baby,

but Jack-Jack managed to cling to his rocket boots. Syndrome spun out of control as Jack-Jack began ripping the boots apart. With a chunk of rocket boot in each hand, Jack-Jack let go and began to fall.

Bob and Helen watched from the ground, helpless. What could they do? Helen quickly stretched herself into a javelin, and with all his Super strength, Bob flung her toward the baby. She soared into the sky but overshot the baby and dove down like a sky diver. The ground was coming up fast when Helen reached out and snatched Jack-Jack out of the air. Billowing out like a parachute, Helen drifted down with the baby in her arms.

"This isn't the end of it!" Syndrome shouted, having regained control. He stood in the docking door of his jet, his cape blowing in the wind. Then Bob reached for his beloved new sports car and flung it into the air.

"I will get your son!" Syndrome shouted as the car hit the jet, knocking him off balance. *"I'll—"*

Then he felt the tug at his neck. He turned in time to see the end of his cape sucked into the jet's turbines. It was his last monologue.

"Look at Mommy, honey," Helen said to baby

Jack-Jack, who had returned to normal in her arms. "Mommy's got you. Everything's all right."

But Jack-Jack saw the burning wreckage of the jet coming toward them. Pointing upward, the terrified baby began to shriek. Helen landed, and the Incredibles huddled together as the debris landed around them, erupting in a massive explosion.

The Parr home was completely destroyed. But inside the wreckage, inches from being crushed, the Incredibles were alive. Vi had created her most powerful force field ever. They looked at her from within the bubble, amazed by her strength.

"That's my girl," Helen said. The family was saved! They walked out of the smoldering wreckage without a scratch.

"Ooohh, man, *that was totally wicked!*" The neighborhood boy on the trike was wowed.

Chapter 32

Things were different for the Parr family from then on. Their Super identities were still secret, but their new confidence wasn't.

"You're . . . Violet, right?" Tony Rydinger said to Vi at the school track meet.

"That's me," Vi answered, holding her head up.

"You look . . . different," Tony said.

"I feel different. Is different okay?"

"Different is great," Tony said, liking the person he saw. "Do you think maybe you and I . . . you know?" Tony stammered, feeling a little shy.

"I like movies." Vi smiled, putting him at ease. "I'll buy the popcorn, okay?"

"A movie," Tony answered. "There you go, yeah . . . yeah! So, Friday?"

"Friday," Violet said with a big smile.

Running in the track meet that day was Dash Parr. His family was in the stands to cheer him on.

"Go! Go, Dash, *go*! Run. Run! *Run!*" Bob, Helen, and Vi yelled after the starting pistol fired.

Dash stayed at the back of the pack and smiled

up at his family.

"Go, Dash, go! Go bigger, don't give up."

Dash accelerated and moved to the front of the pack.

"But not too fast!" Bob and Helen cheered as Dash held back, finishing the race a triumphant second. The Incredible family couldn't have been prouder.

As they all headed for home, a sudden rumble began to shake the parking lot. The ground swelled and then violently broke apart as a massive drilling machine surfaced. Dramatically, a super villain with giant metal claws emerged, shouting, "Behold the Underminer! I am always beneath you, but nothing is beneath me!"

The villain continued to monologue as Bob looked over at Helen, shook his head, and smiled. The family already had their masks on. *This one is going to be easy,* Bob thought as he ripped off his shirt, revealing the *I* for *Incredible* on his Super suit. The Incredibles were ready!